FALLEN PINE CONES

A Novel

Z. T. Balian

Vakr Books
ISBN: 9780997111613

VAKR BOOKS

Cover artwork © Chritch "The Nest" (2012) – www.chritch.com

Website: www.ztbalian.com
Instagram: @balianzt

"*Fallen Pine Cones* is set during the Lebanese war of 1975 and the following decades. The civil war is best summed up in one of the lines in the first chapter in which the complicated war results in the simple division of Beirut into the Christian East and Muslim West – "a simplistic way of dividing a society that was made up of minorities of every creed." Balian weaves a tight story of seven close friends from very different backgrounds, typical of the diversity at the time. Together they traverse a minefield of shifting loyalties, forbidden relationships, love, betrayal, and devastation. It is a marvellous allegory for the ultimate story of a war that was far more unfathomable than a simple division of land; the reverberations of which shaped not just these friends but a whole nation. Beautifully told, we see the human toll of conflict and begin to understand the complex heart and soul of Beirut. It is not just a story of war, but a heartfelt love letter to Lebanon and its people."

Victoria Harwood Butler-Sloss, author of
The Seamstress of Ourfa

"*Fallen Pine Cones* is not only a gripping story about friendship, love, and forgiveness, but also the story of Lebanon's civil war. The novel traces the lives of seven friends, who among themselves represent the diverse composition of the country itself, cutting across sects and ethnicities. It tells the story of the cosmopolitan Lebanon that once existed and may once again exist. It focuses on the resilience of the Lebanese people, whose souls are tested by horrific tragedies, and the ties that continue to bind them wherever the tide of war takes them. The reader is taken back and forth time, and some of the stories are told in flashbacks. The author maintains the pace and the momentum, revealing dark secrets at the very end, which makes for a real page-turner. This is a good read for those looking for a heartwarming love story and also for those seeking to understand one of the most complex countries in the Middle East."

Tanya Goudsouzian, Canadian journalist specialising in
the Middle East and Afghanistan

"Fallen Pine Cones is a captivating rendering of a moving story. Balian's knowledge of the ethos of Beirut and familiarity with the locales of Paris and Hamilton, make it an excellent novel. Compassionately narrated, and set against the background of the Lebanese civil war, it is the gripping story of seven friends, belonging to different factions of Beirut's melting pot, and of their love for each other amidst the horror of violence."

Abie Alexander,
author of *For the Love of Armine*

"Fallen Pine Cones is a poignant tale of a small group of youngsters in the 1970's Beirut, who are thrust into the throes of a brutal war. A civil war that will rob them of their innocence and test them to breaking point."

Annie Hoglind,
author and translator

"Fallen Pine Cones is a compelling novel about how the Lebanese Civil War impacts a group of friends. Skilfully blending the different viewpoints of the protagonists, the story is relayed through a number of flashbacks, each revealing a new aspect of their relationships. And with each new

revelation, the reader is lured into impatiently continuing to read the following chapter. Beautifully written, the novel transports the reader to the dangerous streets of Beirut and the lively streets of Paris as Balian weaves a stirring story which will remain food for thought long after the reading is over."

Sosy Mishoyan, author and academic
(University of Michigan, Ann Arbor)

AUTHOR'S NOTE

This book is dedicated to all those who have suffered from conflicts around the world, who still bear the invisible scars, and whose stories have not yet been told. I am grateful to my first readers and 'listeners', in particular Catherine Keenan and Maral and Asbed Balian, whose advice and suggestions have encouraged me to complete the work. I have had the fortune of having three excellent editors – Jolene and Robert Gear and Ann Newman. I am forever in their debt. I wish to extend a heartfelt thanks to artist Chritch for allowing me to use her painting. And lastly, I would like to thank my family and friends for their support and affection.

For William

"Nothing is lost if we have the courage to proclaim that everything is lost and we must start again."

— Julio Cortázar, *Hopscotch*

CONTENTS

THE SEVEN FRIENDS

Nora – granddaughter of survivors of the Armenian Genocide (who took refuge in Lebanon) belonging to the Armenian Apostolic Church

Carole – granddaughter of Jewish refugees from Bolshevik Russia who converted to Christianity (Evangelical) in Lebanon and changed their surnames

Sana – daughter of a conservative Sunni Islam family

Tony – son of Greek Orthodox parents

Waleed – son of a father from the Druze faith (an Islamic sect) and a Catholic Maronite mother

Ramzi – son of a Shiite Islam family

Michel – son of Greek Catholic parents

CHAPTER 1

THE FEMALE CORPSE

The charred body of a woman lay naked, face down, on the asphalt ground of the now impassable Sin El-Fil Highway, blocked by concrete barriers. The highway followed the path of the dried-up and abandoned Beirut River, linking Sin El-Fil to Bourj Hammoud, areas in the periphery of the city. It was an unusually quiet early afternoon – eerily silent. The autumn rains had arrived but had temporarily given way to an Indian Summer. Seven teenagers stood, stunned, on the long and narrow balcony of a high-rise block, built on the edge of Sioufi Hill in East Beirut. A drop of some 100 metres separated them from the corpse. One of them, agitated, swiftly fetched a pair of binoculars, which they passed around without uttering a word. The cadaver was the colour black: black back, black buttocks, black limbs, black hair – an unnatural frizzy ball. The three teenage girls, terrorized by what they had seen, retreated inside in horror. The boys, a year or two older, reacted in unison and swiftly followed them in. But none of them knew then that their lives would never be the same again after that day.

Everyone was now standing in the middle of the living room, not knowing what to do next. Tony, whose parents owned the apartment, looked at Nora. She was by now familiar with this look – the one he gave her every time he wanted to prompt her to act, to take a decision, or to choose whatever it was that had to be chosen. Nora was the youngest of the teenagers, but for reasons she could not fathom herself, she was, de facto, the leader of the group.

"Michel, go downstairs and check what it's all about with the Christian militia guys in the neighbourhood," she ordered while watching Sana collapse on the plush three-seat sofa.

"My father will kill me if he finds out I'm here," wailed Sana, unable to hide her fear.

"Don't be such a cry baby! Carole and Waleed will take you home as soon as Michel comes back," said Nora.

Ramzi went and sat next to Sana and held her hand to comfort her.

"This is really close," Waleed said. "I've never seen a corpse before, and I'm sure none of you has."

Tony and Carole, standing next to him, nodded in agreement and tried to hide their shock as best they could.

It was true. None of them had seen a corpse like this before. Some of them had witnessed the passing of a grandparent, but nothing like this. During the last three months, they had all experienced the skirmishes in their neighbourhoods with Kalashnikovs or M16s fired from one street to another, the stray bullets, and the RPG rockets that landed pretty much anywhere because they were mostly fired at random. Hell was let loose and the downtown shopping areas were completely destroyed – looted and set alight. The civil war had been akin to a spectacle for them at the beginning. They had not seen any of the atrocities committed with their own eyes. They had only heard of people getting killed for what their identity cards stated they were. Christians kidnapped and killed Muslims, and vice versa.

The civil war had started with the Palestinians killing a group of young Lebanese Christian men, and the Lebanese Christians retaliated in kind. But these incidents divided Lebanese society. The Palestinian Command of the PLO had been given refuge in Lebanon after they were banished in the late 1960's from Jordan where they previously had their base. Upon establishing their headquarters in Beirut, the Palestinians, who were allowed to keep their arms, began to take control of certain areas of the city. The local authorities could not access those neighbourhoods and were no longer in charge of them. By the mid-1970's, international and regional politics were being played out in situ. Thus, those who supported the Palestinians and their presence in the country and those who were against it formed the two opposing camps. And the city of Beirut was divided into two – the 'Christian' East Beirut and the 'Muslim' West Beirut. Just like that – a simplistic way of dividing a society that was made up of minorities of every creed.

For the seven friends, this divide had not been a problem so far. They all came from different backgrounds and different minorities in the country and all still lived at home like all other youngsters of their age, but nothing and nobody was going to put an end to the bond they had forged three years ago. They had managed to get together whenever it was possible, ignoring the Green Line that divided the city. Save for the burnt-out business heart of the city, there was always a crossing route somewhere in the Green Line that was passable. All they had to do was to listen to the reports on Voice of Lebanon radio to ascertain where the passage was. None of them could imagine that the situation in the country could get worse and further restrict their movements.

Nora, Tony, and Michel lived in East Beirut, Carole, Waleed, and Sana in West Beirut. Ramzi lived outside Beirut. What had united them three years ago was their love of music, and specifically, a local radio pop/rock music programme. They were all followers of the female DJ of that programme whose fan base had grown from a few hundred to thousands of teenagers and young adults in a very short period – a new phenomenon never seen in the country before. Confronted with this new reality, the DJ had conjured up the idea of organizing weekend activities for her fans, which involved group games, dance parties, as well as concerts by musicians from abroad. The first time the seven friends met was at a concert played by a Jamaican band. The vast concert hall was teeming with youngsters when Tony, who had brought Michel along, approached Nora with a smile. 'I recognise you. Don't you live in my neighbourhood?' he said and settled on the seat next to hers before she could even answer him. Soon afterwards, Carole and Waleed, who had just begun dating, arrived with Ramzi and Sana and occupied the vacant seats on the other side of Nora's. While waiting for the concert to begin, they soon began to converse and after the concert, too excited by their new discovery of the reggae tunes of the band to call it a night, they all went to a pizza joint. And that was how it all started.

What eventually cemented their friendship was above and beyond their common interest in music though. Over time, they discovered they all had the common vision of an ideal society where people of different backgrounds and persuasions could coexist and benefit from each other. Nora, the headstrong young woman that she was, was the initiator of all the discussions they had. The society they dreamed of was in stark contrast to their reality – a society that focused on separating rather than uniting communities. All seven of them also resented the intrusive nature of the society they lived in and the inertia of their conservative environment. They believed that, with their strong convictions, their generation could bring about the much- needed tolerance, fairness, and openness to everyday life.

The day they saw the corpse, they'd arrived at Tony's to celebrate his 19th birthday. Tony's Greek Orthodox family had lived in East Beirut for generations. Of medium height and with light brown hair, Tony had soft, endearing eyes. Nora had loved those eyes from the moment she looked into them. She was certain he was attracted to her, but neither of them had expressed any sentiments for fear of sounding clumsy. They were both still fairly inexperienced in matters of love and dating. For now, they were content to remain close friends. Tony admired Nora immensely for her intelligence and sense of adventure. For him, she was the most beautiful girl he'd ever come across. She had thick, straight, dark hair that contrasted with her light complexion. Her large, dark eyes, with long eyelashes, were what she had inherited from her Armenian ancestors.

Ramzi was from a Shiite Muslim village in the vicinity of Byblos, the ancient Phoenician town, situated some 36 km north of Beirut. He was considered very handsome by local standards. He was very tall, lean, with blond wavy hair and hazel eyes. He was also the kindest friend one could have. Always ready to help, even at a moment's notice, he was fiercely loyal to his friends. He and Sana had met at one of the first parties organized by the famous radio DJ and immediately clicked. Sana was a petite brunette with smooth olive skin. She had very fine features and delicate hands. It was love at first sight for both of them. But Sana could not openly go out with him. Not only was she a Sunni Muslim, but she also came from a very conservative family, her father having performed the Hajj pilgrimage to Mecca three times.

At this time, Carole and Waleed had been going out for just over three years and were very much in love. Like two peas in a pod, they formed the perfect couple. Carole, a very attractive young lady, was a redhead with green eyes. Her family originally hailed from Russia. Her grandfather was a Russian Jew who had escaped to Lebanon with White Russians when the Bolsheviks took over. A few years after his arrival in Beirut, he had converted to Protestantism, adopted an Arab surname, and married a Jewish woman from the congregation who, like him, had converted to Christianity. Although Carole's Jewish background was not a problem for her grandfather in the old days, it did become a problem for her father, especially after the 1967 Arab-Israeli War that led to the exodus of many Jewish families from Lebanon. Consequently, other than from her closest friends, Carole kept her Jewish connection well-hidden from everyone else.

Waleed had brought his acoustic guitar along for the occasion to sing a few of his friends' favourites. He did an excellent rendition of James Taylor's 'Fire and Rain'. He said it was his birthday gift to Tony. Waleed was a talented musician. None of his friends were in doubt of that. His being an accomplished musician was more obvious when he played the electric guitar. They'd all watched him perform at a concert at his well-known international school two years prior. He even had the look of a rock star – a dark Mick Jagger. He was tall and thin, with long, skinny legs. He always wore jeans. Unlike Jagger though, his dark, thick curly hair almost covered the entirety of his long, thin face. This gave him an air of mystery, someone difficult to access. He felt at ease with his group of friends but not with anyone outside the group. He was an introvert and people generally found him to be aloof and accused him of being a snob. Waleed was the offspring of a Christian mother, a Maronite, and a Druze father, an unusual union in Lebanon. Given the current circumstances, this served his purpose for being able to cross the Green Line in his VW Beetle without much bother. He had two identification cards – his real one that mentioned his sectarian affiliation with the Druze, his father's sect being the one recognized by the law, and his fake one that his mother had procured the previous month. As a child, she'd had him baptized according to the Maronite Catholic rite. She was thus able to convince a 'mukhtar' (local municipal representative) to issue Waleed with papers identifying him as a Christian Maronite.

Michel, a Greek Catholic, was Tony's neighbour. He lived on the first floor of the same building with his parents and his much older, half-brother. His father's first wife had died of illness at a young age. Michel, the offspring of a second marriage, didn't get along with his half-brother whom he loathed. The mutual hatred between the two half-siblings was a reality neither his parents nor his friends could grasp fully. Michel regarded Tony as his true brother instead. Tony was his mentor and his best friend. Being inherently of a shy nature, it had taken Michel some time to completely feel at ease with his group of friends. He considered himself lucky to be part of the group and had grown to love each and every one of them. And he was flattered by the attention the girls gave him. They often mothered him for he was of small stature and had a cute baby face.

It was a good half hour before Michel came back. He was heaving. He had perspired so much his hair was stuck to his head in wet strands. Sweat beads covered his entire flushed face. He looked as if he'd run a full day's marathon.

"She was a Palestinian woman," he said almost on the verge of tears. "The Christian militia caught her spying. They interrogated her and she confessed she'd been sent by the Palestinian Command based in the Tel Zaatar Camp to spy on their activities. They killed her afterwards, burnt her body, and then dumped it on the highway."

Autumn 1975 – that was forty years ago. Nora still remembered the day as if it was yesterday. She could see the faces of her six friends as if they were standing right in front of her now. She must have been dreaming, or maybe, she had dozed off, she thought. Bit by bit, life had chipped away the precious joy they had felt before that fateful day. That happiness had gradually been replaced with individual and collective tragedies. She suddenly checked her watch. It was time to go to the waiting lounge for the flight from Paris to Toronto. Take off was in an hour.

She got up and headed towards the waiting lounge, still uncertain as to why she was going ahead with this trip. She could not bring herself to say no to Tony. Yes, she felt betrayed – still after all these years. But this was a matter beyond any betrayal or grudge. This was the plea of a dying friend. Why does life have to put one in front of such difficult and sad situations? That's what she thought as she finally boarded the plane and settled in her seat. She suddenly thought she could smell Tony's perfume – an old-fashioned French scent that was trendy at the time. It brought up the image of the two of them dancing to a slow tune at one of their parties in Beirut. Why was she dwelling on the past? She quickly banished the thought. It was of no use being over-emotional about the past. Still, it was hurtful that Tony and Carole had practically forgotten about her. They did send her a Christmas card every year, without fail. The contents were a couple of lines expressing best wishes but very little about their lives. She knew they had a son named Paul. She had not even seen a single picture of him, not even as a baby. He would probably be 37 now.

Over the years Tony and Carole had called her only twice since she'd last seen them in Paris. Once to congratulate her on the birth of her daughter and once to express condolences on the passing of both her parents, which occurred in the same year. After they immigrated to Canada, she had decided to forgive them, Tony in particular. She had convinced herself that it was for the best. Initially, she'd regularly written letters to them, giving them her latest news about her life in Paris. But when they did not reciprocate, she resorted to only sending them season's greetings once a year and a few pictures of her daughter as she was growing up.

The phone call from Tony came out of the blue one Sunday afternoon. When she heard his voice, it was so unexpected it almost left her breathless. Her long-buried heartache immediately returned, but she chose to ignore it. He was his old warm self – as always, soft spoken, polite, and considerate. As he spoke, she felt as if he had always been by her side and had never gone away. She then was taken aback when he told her he was sending her a plane ticket to come to Canada. She could set the dates that were convenient for her. He said he would pick her up at Toronto Pearson International Airport and drive to Hamilton. Tony and Carole had lived there since they first got to Canada 38 years ago.

"We both want you to come," he said. "It's Carole's last wish."

"What? What do you mean?"

"She's been in hospital for the last month. She has lung cancer and she doesn't have much time," he said, his voice cracking. "We need to see you."

CHAPTER 2

SAINT BALASH

It was going to be a long flight. Nora closed her eyes and tried to remember the happy times in Lebanon, before the civil war. Nostalgia was not the correct word when recalling those happy times. It was stronger than mere nostalgia. Those happy times were what had forged her character and made her who she was today. The first image that came to her mind was the seven of them at a free beach which they had named Saint Balash, 'balash' meaning 'for free' in Arabic. Saint Balash made sense as on route to this beach, on the northern coastal road from Beirut, there were paying beach clubs with names like Saint Vincent or Saint John or some other saint's name. All seven of them regularly frequented those paying beaches as well, usually with their parents or siblings, in the summer season which extended from mid-April to the end of September, just before schools re-opened. That was the norm with the middle and wealthy classes in Lebanon. But this was different. It was their secret beach location that could not be shared with others. Nora could almost smell the Mediterranean just by thinking about Saint Balash. When she was growing up in Beirut, she could not imagine not living near the sea, and yet, she had spent the best part of the last forty years in Paris, away from the sea.

How she missed that alluring beach. The white, soft sand and the pristine turquoise water that was so irresistible. The water urged one to jump in. Even though she'd been on holiday to many other beaches in other countries, nothing could match the one just past the town of Byblos. Being from the area, it was Ramzi who had found the deserted spot on the beach. Once a week in the summer, the beach trip was one activity none of them wanted to miss. They'd go prepared. There would be enough food for breakfast and lunch. Sana was the only one in the group who couldn't swim and acted as the 'hostess' in setting the 'table' while the others went swimming. She would bring 'kunafa bi-jibn', the breakfast sweet made with semolina and unsalted white cheese, sandwiched in a sesame seed covered small, round loaf of bread. Tony and Michel were the masters of 'manakeesh', the pizza-like breakfast Lebanese staple with an olive-oil mixture of crushed wild thyme, spices, and sesame seeds as topping. They both knew which bakeries made the best ones and also which made the best cheese turnovers. Nora herself would bring anything that her mum was willing to make – hummus, 'tabboule', aubergine caviar, and sometimes Armenian stuffed vine leaves. Carole always brought the condiments – pickles, olives, and turnips. They'd buy tomatoes, cucumbers, strained yogurt, and Lebanese large flat loaves on the way. As soon as they arrived in Byblos, their meeting point with Ramzi, he'd be waiting for them with a cooler loaded with soft drinks and Lebanese pilsner beer.

Waleed would take care of the musical entertainment part. He always brought his acoustic guitar along and his battery-operated turn-table with some of his LPs. Nora remembered well how they all saved their pocket money to be able to buy vinyl records.

"What shall I play first?" Waleed would say, turning to Nora.

Nora was always the honorary DJ. She was the most knowledgeable amongst them when it came to music. She knew all the latest trends in music and was passionate about it. Every night she'd take her small transistor radio to bed and listen to various music programmes, especially the BBC ones, in succession. Sometimes, if she was able to capture the correct frequency, she'd listen to the pirate radio programmes that were broadcast from ships off the coast of Beirut.

"Let's start with 'Guinevere'. That'll put us in a good mood," she'd say to Waleed.

They'd begin with Crosby, Stills, and Nash, followed by Jethro Tull, King Crimson, Pink Floyd, Joni Mitchell, and finally, Genesis. In between short swims and bites to eat, they'd pour over the lyrics of 'Selling England by the Pound' with excitement. Nora thought how lucky she was to have lived her teenage years in that era. Looking back on those years, she had no regrets that she and her friends were not all that interested in Arabic music. Not because it wasn't interesting, but because Arabic music was naturally a part of their daily lives, something they took for granted. Fairuz and Um Kalthum songs were played everywhere – in restaurants, in 'sérvice' shared taxis, in clubs, on TV. These Arabic songs were part of their DNA. The same was true of French music – the whole range, from Charles Aznavour to Jacques Brel, was heard every day and everywhere. Nora was also proud of her cosmopolitan upbringing. Although Lebanon was a small country, it was the only truly open Arab society she could think of. Her being exposed to different cultures while growing up had made her a more tolerant person and given her a bit of an edge over others, she felt.

Nora smiled to herself at the thought of Lebanon being the 'Switzerland of the Middle East'. That's how it was advertised to tourists. It was all true then. Thinking about it now, she felt sad. Lebanon lured not only the European or American tourists, but also the glamorous rich and famous, the jet setters, the journalists and the Cold War spies. She remembered the tourist brochure of the mid-1960's she'd seen as a child that said you could go to the beach in the morning and ski in the mountains of Lebanon in the afternoon. There were two pictures on the brochure: a blonde model in a bikini water-skiing near the famous Saint Georges Hotel in Beirut and the same model skiing on a snow-covered slope somewhere up in the mountains. That was also true. But why on earth would anyone want to do that? She never understood the concept. If you went to the beach, it was for a full day's enjoyment. If you went to the mountains, you also needed a full day to enjoy it.

She remembered well how, depending on how much money they had, she and her friends would go to a fish restaurant overlooking Jounieh Marina on the way back to Beirut from 'their' beach. They didn't want the beach day to end. They all felt a full day had to be a full day. They'd have crispy, fried Sultan Ibrahim, small red mullets, the taste of which Nora was never able to replicate even if she found red mullets at the fish market in Paris.

Now and again, the seven friends would organize a day's outing to the Metn Mountains for the cooler air to escape Beirut's unbearable heat in August. For this, they didn't have to worry about taking food with them. They'd drive up to one of the villages north of Bikfaya and have a copious village breakfast there that included fresh farm eggs fried in individual deep terracotta plates, local cheese, and vegetables. They would then go for a long walk in the fresh air in a pine forest until late afternoon. Her eyes now closed Nora felt transported to that place in time. She could smell the flowers and the wild thyme. She could hear the sound of the cicadas in the summer heat. She could see the majestic pine trees shading them from the sunlight – the trees that Tony loved so much.

Later in the early evening, the group would eventually end up in one of the hip villages that were frequented by the Beirut crowds in the summer and where it was essential to see and be seen. Crowds of Beirutis would be pacing up and down the main road of the village for their supposed evening exercise. But in reality, the young girls and boys would be seeking to find that summer love amongst the crowd and the older ones would be looking to impress acquaintances with their new summer attires or hairdos. Old folks would be sitting at the outdoor cafés smoking their 'argilehs', water-pipes, while chatting away. At one of the cafés/restaurants which the seven friends frequented and which only came alive in the summer, they'd invariably have a homemade burger with the thinnest hand-cut French fries. They'd end the evening meal with a 'Chocolat

Mou', chocolate ice cream served in a tall glass, topped with chocolate sauce and Chantilly cream.

When the rains came in October, and school started, they'd prepare themselves for weekend outings to the cinema. They never missed a new Truffaut, a Kubrick, or a Fellini movie which were shown in their original, usually uncensored, versions in cinemas in the Hamra area of Beirut. After the movie, they'd go to a small café off the main street of Hamra and spend hours discussing the film. This was also the area where they went shopping for clothing, records, books, and foreign magazines. Nora reminisced about the excitement of finding tucked away boutiques that sold the trendiest fashions that came from Paris or London, and about buying her first non-school book. It was Beckett's *Waiting for Godot*. The play so overwhelmed her that she felt obligated to share her excitement with her friends.

She now wondered how they could afford such a relatively luxurious lifestyle on their meagre pocket money. How times have changed, she thought. Other than Waleed, whose father was a very wealthy businessman, the rest of them came from low-middle class or middle-class families. Yet, all of them went to private schools which were bi-lingual or tri-lingual institutions. Not that all Lebanese government-run schools were bad. They also offered a bi-lingual curriculum and some of their students had excellent results in school-leaving exams. In Lebanon, it was a matter of how families prioritized their children's education and how attached they were to the idea of entrusting their children's education to their specific communities. And, other than the few prestigious schools like Waleed's international school, the tuition fees of normal private schools were affordable at the time. Most of these schools were run by associations representing the different communities in the country, and scholarship offers to children whose families could not afford the payments were common.

Nora herself went to an Armenian school run by the Armenian community. Tony went to the local Greek Orthodox-run high school. Michel went to a school run by Catholic priests and Ramzi, who had started at a government-run school, finished high school at a private school in Byblos. Sana went to a Catholic school run by nuns. When asked why her religious Sunni father sent her to a Christian school, she matter-of-factly said he liked the discipline that the nuns inculcated in students. Carole, who was on a partial scholarship because of her high grades, went to the prestigious Protestant school for girls. During the two years prior to the start of hostilities, all seven of them had finished high school and had gone to university except for Michel, who was enrolled on an accounting course at a technical college.

Tony, Waleed, and Ramzi had completed their sophomore year at the American University of Beirut and Nora, Carole, and Sana had finished their freshman year at the same institution when the fighting started in September, interrupting the opening of schools and universities. Ramzi was studying nursing. Sana, not knowing what else to do, had chosen nursing as well, mainly to be able to see him on a daily basis. Waleed majored in architecture and Tony in mechanical engineering. Carole, undecided between biology and economics, followed Nora's lead and became a business administration student. With the civil war raging, they would all lose a whole academic year.

The flight attendant, pushing a trolley full of all types of drinks, brought Nora back to the present when she halted in front of Nora's aisle and asked her what she wanted to drink. Nora ordered a whiskey and water. As she took the first sip, she saw with her mind's eye the bottle of Johnny Walker Red Label that Waleed and Tony had bought for the snow trip. In the winter, a trip to the snowy slopes of Faraya was what they all looked forward to. The last time they'd been there was in February, a few months before the civil war broke out. They'd set out in two cars, Waleed's VW Beetle and Ramzi's old Renault. None of them could ski, except for Waleed. He went on a winter ski trip with his parents to Switzerland or Austria at least once a year. He owned one of the newly-invented pairs of fibreglass skis. In Faraya village shops though, one could only find the old-fashioned wooden ones. On that trip, the boys hired them and Waleed taught them the basics of skiing for the first time. And it was on that trip that the whiskey bottle was drunk – all of it! Back then, no one had the notion of not drinking and driving. And none of them had any notion of the dangers they faced with cars that had no chains on their tires when they drove on hair-spinning, slippery bends of mountain slopes covered in snow. But they didn't care.

Nora had another sip of her whiskey and her mind then turned to springtime in Lebanon. Spring brought with it the invitation to visit the Bekaa Valley, in the east of the country. The last time they all went, they decided to take only two cars again, and Tony was glad not to have to drive his newly-bought, second-hand, tiny Fiat. He wasn't quite confident it would be suitable for a long journey out of Beirut. The early morning ride to the Bekaa Valley passed through some of the finest countryside of the land where one could spot the new, wild blossoms and the odd shepherd with his flock of black mother goat and her kids. The mountain route that descended towards the valley offered them a spectacular bird's eye view of the vast farmland below. Every time they'd been to the Bekaa Valley, they'd made sure it was a true feast day, and this time was no exception. When they reached the first big town, Chtaura, they stopped at one of the shops that sold fresh dairy products. Here, they had the famed local country thin bread sandwich with strained yogurt, olive oil, and fresh mint for breakfast.

They then continued on to Anjar, the small town that was built by Armenian refugees who had settled there in the 1920's and who were known for their immaculate fruit orchards. Open-air restaurants, next to a quietly flowing brook, dotted the centre of town. There, they chose a table shaded by enormous trees, at one of the restaurants to have lunch. The array of appetizers, the mezze, was so varied that by the time the main course arrived everyone was already full.

On that day, they all had too much to eat and drink. Going back to Beirut that evening, Nora and Tony, tipsy as they were, huddled in the back seat of Waleed's VW Beetle. The sun had not quite set, and light and shade rivalled each other. Tony gave Nora her first kiss – just a quick peck – but a kiss nevertheless.

CHAPTER 3
KARANTINA

*Murder has changed the city's shape – this stone
is a child's head –
and this smoke is exhaled from human lungs
from "Desert" by Adonis (trans. from the Arabic by
Khaled Matawwa)*

I t was a cold January afternoon in 1976 when they were
forcibly brought to the government school, perhaps the
largest in the area, which had remained shut since the
beginning of the school year. It was adjacent to the building
where Nora lived. There was commotion in the neighbourhood, and even though it was freezing cold, the neighbours
were all out on their balconies. No one said a word. Everyone watched. From her vantage point of her family's apartment balcony on the fourth floor, she could see the vast
school yard, a section of the school building, and part of
the entrance to the school. Some arrived in buses, which

went through the gate and disappeared somewhere in the lower entrails of the colossal school building. The bus windows were blacked out. She could not tell who was on board. Others arrived on foot, guarded by armed Christian militia. They were mainly women and children and a few old men. They had nothing with them. There were no belongings, no bags. Some of them wore their traditional garb and many had no shoes on. They looked absolutely terrified. She noticed some of the women and children were crying but she could not hear them and neither could she hear the instructions they were given by the militiamen, which the 'prisoners' sheepishly followed. It was clear to Nora that they feared for their lives. They formed a long queue and were herded into the school building.

'The remaining population of Karantina', she heard her older brother say. He'd been standing next to her and she hadn't noticed. 'Look!' He pointed to the area south west of their location, towards Beirut Port. Her neighbourhood stood on a hill to the east of Karantina. It overlooked Karantina but was not close enough for her to make out the roads and houses. She could clearly see the winter grey sea though, but it was greyer that day with the thick smoke rising from the Karantina area.

She knew what Karantina meant. It was a slum which housed poor refugees and squatters. These were Kurds and Syrians, who had fled Turkey and Syria, but the majority was Palestinian. Karantina was initially a refugee camp built by the French under whom Lebanon was mandated after the First World War. Its original purpose was to house the first wave of Armenian refugees who arrived in the country in 1920. They were the survivors of the Machiavellian plan of the Young Turks to annihilate their race and wipe them off the surface of their very own lands. They were seen as Christian traitors and an obstacle to the survival of a new Turkish Muslim state. Many of these Armenian refugees were talented artisans and skilled workers. The French encouraged them to move out of the camp a few years later. Most of them succeeded in getting out of the slum in a matter of 6 years. They spread out to the neighbouring areas, and in particular Bourj Hammoud, where they established small businesses. They soon built schools and churches and created a new life for themselves in Lebanon.

Nora's grandparents were also survivors of the Armenian Genocide. They were housed not in Karantina but in another French refugee camp when they first arrived in Lebanon. They stayed there for a short while before moving to the Ashrafieh area where her parents and Nora herself were born and where they still lived.

"What do you mean by the remaining population of Karantina?"

"They're talking about massacre on a large scale. There's talk of rape, too. They've torched the entire place," her brother said, looking concerned.

"I can't believe this is happening. These are poor refugees. They're helpless. They're like our grandparents were only 50 years ago."

"Yes, but they've been harbouring the Palestinian, Muslim, and leftist militia in Karantina," she heard her father say. He was now standing at the threshold of the balcony.

She knew that, too. During the last months there were skirmishes every day. The Palestinians and their allies would be firing towards her neighbourhood and the

Christian militia would fire back. Or, it would be the other way around. One couldn't tell who started first. The fighting had intensified recently and people were getting killed. In her neighbourhood, the victims were mainly civilians. A rocket would land next to people walking or shopping. A stray bullet had killed a woman two blocks away when she'd gone on the roof of the building to hang her washing.

"There have been too many casualties of recent. I can't blame the Christian militia. Something had to be done about Karantina," her father continued. "There are forces trying their best to split us, the Armenians, too. A small number of pro-Palestinian Armenians had joined those in Karantina. We're supposed to remain neutral in this conflict, so that's really not acceptable."

Her father was getting angrier as he spoke. Nora didn't want to contradict him. He had lost his business. His tiny jewellery shop in downtown Beirut was completely destroyed and the contents looted. He'd been at home without work for months now. He'd been using his savings to ensure that his family survived these tough times. And no one knew when they would end.

"See this?" Her father now pointed to the bullet lodged in one of their balcony's wooden shutters.

It was a stray bullet that had penetrated the shutter a couple of weeks ago. Half of the bullet was visible. Her father put his index finger on it.

"This is a dum-dum bullet. If it penetrates your body, it will explode inside you. Come, let's go to the kitchen," he continued, dragging her in. "The hole made by the same kind of bullet on the side of your mum's cooker *is* real. She could have been killed while cooking. Do you understand that? Something had to be done about Karantina. This is war. You either have to kill or be killed."

Nora remained silent, again not wanting to start an argument with her father. She couldn't help it. She felt sorry for the refugees holed up in the school. They looked pitiful. They needed help. What was going to be their fate? Nora couldn't sleep well that night. How could she when they were so close? What were the Christian militia doing to them? Nora thought she heard car noises but she couldn't be sure. She kept on waking up every now and again until she could see daylight. She got up. She found her father sitting at the dining table, his head in his hands. He looked up when he heard her shuffle.

"They killed 1000. There were civilians and fighters. They didn't make the distinction."

"What about the people here, in the school? I saw buses come in yesterday. Who were in those buses?" she asked.

"Probably the younger women they'd captured. And don't ask me what they've done to them. I really don't know and have no way of finding out," he said, angry and agitated.

"What happened to all these people? And the children? Did they kill them?" Nora said in a quiet voice trying very hard to hide her emotions.

"The ones who were brought to the school were spared – I think. Old buses came in an hour ago and they were taken away. They're out of this area. They are now refugees again, but somewhere else," he said with great sadness.

Two weeks later, there was another atrocity. The town of Damour, 20 km south of Beirut, was attacked by the Palestinian forces and their allies. Some of the townspeople managed to flee, but 500 Christians, mainly civilians, were massacred in cold blood.

"Can you give blood? Someone is in desperate need of your blood type at the Armenian hospital in Bourj Hammoud," said a voice at the other end of the line.

"Sure. I'll be there in 15 minutes," Nora replied.

At the Armenian Club, attached to her neighbourhood church, a special medical unit had been created to cater for the needs of the community when the fighting began. The unit possessed the only ambulance available for the Armenians in the areas of Ashrafieh and Bourj Hammoud, and Nora's brother was one of a group of young Armenians manning it. Nora gave her blood at the medical dispensary there and asked who it was for.

"It's for a pregnant Armenian woman who was shot in the thigh this morning in Bourj Hammoud. We'll be dispatching the blood right now. She's being operated on as we speak," said the nurse.

"Will she make it, do you think?"

"Don't know," came the reply.

"She will surely make it. Can I visit her tomorrow if the operation is successful?"

"Suit yourself," the nurse said and thanked Nora.

The next morning Nora went to the hospital. She had worried all day and night about how this lady was doing. Had she pulled through? Were they able to save her baby? Nora didn't even know her name but she asked around. The pregnant woman had made it she was told and Nora was directed to her room. She was happy to see the lady was awake. She was even happier to see that the bed covers had taken the shape of her protruding belly. She must have been at least six or seven months pregnant.

"How are you doing this morning, madam? My name is Nora," she blurted out as she approached the patient's bed.

"I'm alright. And my baby's fine," she said, touching her bump.

"I'm glad you're okay."

"The bullet entered from one side of my thigh and exited from the other side. But thank God! The surgeon said it didn't damage the bone," the young mother-to-be volunteered the information without being asked. She seemed in a good mood despite the pain which she expressed by wincing now and again.

"That must have been very painful. I'm really sorry that you have to go through this. I wish you a speedy recovery," said Nora and was ready to leave.

"I know you gave me your blood. Your name was mentioned with two others on the paper the club people sent me this morning. Thank you. May God bless you and keep you safe."

Nora nodded, smiled at the lady and then took her leave.

When she got home, she told the story to her brother.

"She's one lucky lady," he said. "Others haven't been. Too many Armenians have been killed these last couple of months. At the club, they're saying that we, the Armenians, have to do something about the situation in Nabaa, which is mainly populated by Palestinian refugees. The Armenians in Bourj Hammoud are caught in the middle, between the

Christian militia who fire from the heights of Ashrafieh and the Palestinian militia who fire back from Nabaa down below, an area practically stuck to Bourj Hammoud. There's serious talk of an imminent plan by the Christian militia to attack and completely over-run the Nabaa area. That would be a disaster. It would be another Karantina. But this time, the scale of the massacre would be far greater."

A week after the conversation Nora had with her brother, the Armenians were finally forced to take action. Not being able to tolerate more Armenian civilian casualties, the Armenians, like Nora's brother predicted, took the initiative and decided to put an end to the precarious situation. The Armenians wished to remain neutral in the conflict but this operation was needed to stop further casualties and prevent further atrocities from being committed. First, the Armenians got assurances from the Christian militia that they would not attack Nabaa and that they would not interfere with the aftermath of the Armenian offensive. The Armenians then attacked the Palestinian militia, who were caught by surprise, and took over their military posts within one week. Some Palestinian militants were killed during the process, some managed to flee, but many gave themselves up. During that week, the Armenians took over one street at a time. Palestinian civilians, now under their control, were taken to the closest Armenian Church to ensure their protection. Once the fighting was over, the Armenians contacted the Palestinian Command to coordinate the process of handing over the Palestinian civilians along with the fighters who had given themselves up. On the set date, all the Palestinians, under Armenian protection, were put on buses and taken to the Green Line where they were handed over to the Palestinian Command.

It was Nora's brother who recounted this to her as he'd been in Bourj Hammoud for part of that week driving the ambulance.

"My heart breaks for all these poor refugees. Being refugees over and over again," she told him.

"But they're alive, not dead. That would certainly have been the case if we hadn't intervened to stop a certain massacre."

"Were the civilians harmed in any way? You know what I mean."

"I can assure you no one even touched a single hair on their heads. Once they were handed over, the Palestinian Command sent the Armenians a message of gratitude for the way they'd handled the situation. I am certain they had intelligence that the Christian militia was ready to over-run Nabaa," he said.

All this murderous chaos was playing in Nora's head. It was worse than any horror movie she had ever watched. This was real. But the memory of the bad times went hand in hand with the good times when she thought of life in Beirut. The humanity and inhumanity of man. She hadn't thought about any of this in years. She wanted to forget the pain and what was lost. Now it all came back to her like a chronic illness that cannot be cured.

'Fasten your seat belts. We have begun our descent to Toronto Pearson International Airport', the announcement interfered with her train of thought and put a halt to her reminiscing about the past. She buckled up and thought of Tony again. She didn't know exactly what was waiting for her in Canada, but she had to remain strong.

CHAPTER 4
THE HASHEESH BALL

The memory of his very first kiss with Nora had never left Tony. It was buried deep inside him. How could he forget that first kiss with the one woman he had ever truly loved in his life? He remembered it now as he got out of the shower at home, having spent the whole night at the hospital. Paul had said he'd relieve him and would go to the hospital in the early morning while he went to pick up Nora from the airport. Tony had taken time off from work to attend to his wife's needs and to be with her. The last few months had been tough on all three of them. He just couldn't stand seeing Carole suffer. But she had been very brave even when the combination treatment of radiotherapy and chemotherapy was awful and her chance of survival minimal. He didn't think he would have been as courageous as she was.

He suddenly panicked. How was he supposed to handle the meeting with Nora? Did he have the strength to go through with it all? He had longed to see her and speak to her face-to-face for the last 38 years. But it had not been possible. Not with things as they were – until now. Difficult as it was at times for both him and Carole, they had over the years, developed a symbiotic relationship not devoid of sincere affection. And he'd been a faithful husband and still was and would be as he had promised Carole – 'till death do us part'.

He'd given Carole a comfortable life although the first three years in Canada were a real struggle for both of them. Caring for the baby took all her time. He had to work part-time to make ends meet and attend university as well to finish his degree. The baby woke up so often at night that Carole would practically be up all night. He'd be up very late, too, studying and could sleep no more than three or four hours every night. But Hamilton, not as lively and exciting as nearby Toronto, where his sister lived, turned out to be a good choice for them. As soon as he graduated, he found a job at one of the largest aluminium factories in the country and moved very quickly up the ladder in the company. Carole didn't have to work. His earnings were more than enough to cover all their needs. She was happy being a homemaker. And in a matter of a few years, he was able to afford to buy her dream home in the sought-after mountain area of Hamilton.

Tony found himself thinking about Nora again. The bond they had forged when they were just teenagers could never be broken. Their friendship was for life. He was certain of that. He needed to draw his strength from Nora. That's what he needed to do at this very trying time. She would make him understand better, cope better with Carole's tragic situation. He genuinely believed Nora would. She was always on his mind even with the passing years. She was always there – in his heart. He hoped she had forgiven him. He hoped she would finally understand why he had married Carole even if he couldn't tell her the whole truth. As twisted as things may have seemed, he'd married Carole to spare Nora all the ugliness that led to the marriage. And it was Carole who had insisted on seeing Nora. Carole had never openly asked him about his feelings for Nora, not even once, but he knew that deep down she was aware of how he felt. 'I want to go with my conscience clear', she'd said and begged him to call Nora.

'I need to be positive', he kept repeating to himself as he got dressed to go to the airport. His mind now wandered again. How happy they all were during that year, before the start of the war, at the American University of Beirut. Even though they had different majors, the six of them met before the semester started to figure out which elective courses they could take together. The first one was a psychology course and the second was a sociology course. Both courses had been fun because of his friends. They'd study for the tests and exams together, and once the studying was over, they'd have the perfect excuse to celebrate by going out to a restaurant or ordering takeaways and having a party at the house of one of them. They'd always make sure to invite Michel, who did not attend university, to come along as they did not wish him to feel excluded from the group.

It was at one of these parties, around the end of the academic year, that Waleed showed them his hasheesh ball. Waleed's parents were away and he had the apartment all to himself for a whole month. None of them had seen, let alone used, hasheesh before.

"I want to show you something spectacular. Here it is. A ball of hasheesh," Waleed said in his usual cool manner. He was holding a round mass, slightly larger than a tennis ball. It was brown in colour and looked as if it was made of clay.

"Here – touch it, pass it around," he said to Tony. They all complied. It was soft to the touch. It seemed malleable like play dough.

"Where did you get that?" Nora inquired, somewhat disturbed.

"From the guys in the neighbourhood. It's the best in the world – fresh from the Bekaa Valley," said Waleed.

"Let's try to smoke some," said Ramzi, his eyes shining with excitement.

And they did. Waleed cut a small piece with his fingernail and placed it in cigarette paper with some tobacco. With great dexterity he rolled it and then lit it. Closing his eyes, he took a second, long drag and passed it on. The girls and Michel barely took a puff each. They wrinkled their noses, coughed, and refused to go any further. Tony took two or three drags and then couldn't remember what happened afterwards. It was only later that he found out.

"You're a silly boy," Nora told him the next day, standing in the lobby of Waleed's spacious apartment.

"Do tell me what happened. I can't remember a thing. Who took you home?"

"I'll tell you what happened," she said, looking really angry. "You and Ramzi went crazy! Ramzi was dancing like a madman and you were out on the balcony trying to fly! That's what happened. Didn't know how to control you – you were going to jump off the balcony! You could have died..." and she burst into tears.

"I'm really, really sorry. Please don't cry."

"Promise you'll never touch that stuff again," she said, wiping her tears.

"I promise."

"Alright then," she murmured. "Michel took us girls home after we made sure Ramzi had stopped dancing, and had collapsed on the sofa, and after we dragged you in and put you to bed. You were in a deep sleep and snoring when we checked ten minutes later. I came back this morning to check up on you."

Just at that moment Waleed appeared with puffy eyes and his curly hair all over the place.

"And you!" Nora said raising her voice. "You'll have to get rid of that shit. It's too potent. I swear I won't speak to you again if I ever see you using it."

"Okay...Okay... Take it easy, don't shout," Waleed said in his usual calm voice and then smiled to himself.

"And wipe that silly smirk off you face – this is no joke." She couldn't help blurting out the words, but Waleed had already disappeared, not wanting to be the object of her wrath.

That was the first ever time sharp words were directed to anyone in the group. But this was Nora and her words counted.

"Trust me, it was not the first time he's used hasheesh. Last night you and Ramzi went nuts but he didn't. He sat there, playing his guitar, as cool as a cucumber. Please Tony, talk to him. Get him off this horrible stuff. Will you?"

"I will do, but please don't discuss this issue with Carole. You will only upset her. And we don't want to be the cause of a row between Waleed and Carole, do we?"

Tony now looked at himself in the mirror. He combed his salt and pepper hair. He was nearly 60 years old. Nora would still be able to recognize him. Just for that he was happy he hadn't gone bald with age.

He left the house feeling confident and happy in anticipation of seeing Nora. But when he started the car, he felt the panic returning. 'God, please help me', he said to himself and put his foot on the accelerator. He drove slowly, trying to calm his nerves. 'Think of the good times', he said to himself. He turned on the radio. An old love song was playing. It transported him to a time when he held Nora in his arms for the first time at a party in Beirut and they danced all night. Afterwards, he spent days kicking himself for not kissing her. She was so close. Her body was soft and warm. Every time her hair touched his face, his knees weakened and he hoped she couldn't notice.

He had felt for some time that he had fallen for her and that she was the one for him. He'd had crushes on girls before, but Nora was different. He didn't want to falter. He had to tread carefully before he made any moves. Relationships with girls had to be given time to mature with the accepted societal norms. That's how things were then in Lebanon. Anything to do with sex was generally taboo, too. No one discussed it openly and especially not with parents. Some years ago, he had opened Paul's bedroom door one morning wanting to ask him something and had found him with the girl he was going out with then. They were both naked in bed. He had apologized to them for the intrusion. This would never have happened to him. His Middle Eastern parents would probably have thrown him out of the house if he'd done something like that and disowned him for good measure. In the old country, for young men like him sexual encounters did take place, either with a lover or a prostitute, but they were well concealed from everyone, with the exception of very close friends, and from parents in particular.

The traffic to the airport was light and Tony got there earlier than he expected. He parked the car and waited until it was time to go to the Arrivals Hall.

"You're a fool. Don't you know I love you? I've always loved you."

Those were the last words Nora had uttered during their last encounter in Paris, shortly before he left for Canada. She was crying and he froze. He couldn't respond to her. He turned around and left. It was the cruellest of acts. He had acted cruelly towards her and towards himself. But he could not have behaved otherwise – under the circumstances. He went to the park nearby and cried silently. His tears flowed uncontrollably and he didn't fight them. He stayed there until it was dark and he was shivering. A few weeks later, he wrote her a letter saying that he'd married Carole and that he was taking her to Canada with him. He asked for her forgiveness and hoped she would understand that he had fallen in love with Carole. He said he cherished Nora's friendship and wished they would remain friends forever. After he got to Canada, he wrote to her again and gave her their address, desperately hoping she would write back. He didn't hear from her for six months, but then a letter arrived. It was written in a friendly manner as if that last encounter between them had never taken place. She wrote about her life in Paris and sounded like the Nora he'd always known.

'She's one tough cookie', Tony thought. She had raised a child as a single mother. She earned good money and had all the confidence he knew he partly lacked. Although he was successful in his career in Hamilton, but unlike her, he could never have made it in a big city such as Paris. He didn't possess her boldness and strength. And he was sure she had a happier life without him. When he left for Canada, he had so longed for her to forget him even if he himself couldn't forget her. It was better that way. He now realized he had developed a cold sweat. Excited about seeing her again after all these years, he also feared it. But he owed it to her and it had to be done. He got out of the car and headed towards Arrivals.

He saw her before she could see him. She had the same shoulder length hair as when she was a lot younger. Her hair was dyed in a lighter shade than her natural hair. She was fuller than he last saw her and slightly overweight which suited her fine. Her face was fuller, too, but she had aged well. She was still an attractive woman and trendily dressed like she always was in her younger days. When he looked at her beautiful dark eyes, they were the same as he remembered them. That's when she recognized him. She walked towards him and opened her arms wide. She gave him a bear hug followed by three kisses on the cheeks like the Lebanese do.

"Aw…Tony! I can't believe I'm here," she said and stepping back she added, "Look at you! You look great! You haven't aged one bit!"

He knew why she said those words. She didn't want to burst into tears. That was her way of controlling her emotions.

"I have aged," he said with a smile. "Look at my grey hair."

"Oh, we've both aged," she said. "It's been 38 long years."

"Yes, too long."

"How is Carole doing? Any new developments regarding her condition?"

"The doctors are not hopeful. Her cancer is quite advanced. But they're trying a new, experimental treatment. It might prolong her life but for how long only God knows."

"I'm really sorry, Tony."

He carried her bag to the car and asked her if she'd like something to eat before they drove to Hamilton. She said she was given breakfast an hour before the plane landed.

"I know a great café in Toronto. I'm guessing you still like your coffee strong, don't you?"

"I'm game," she said. "Those onboard coffees are like brown-coloured hot water. I could do with a double espresso."

Before he started the car, he looked at her face, not believing she was sitting next to him.

"I *am* very happy to see you, Nora. Thank you for coming."

"Now stop it," she said, embarrassed. "You're only going to make me cry."

CHAPTER 5
TONY'S FIAT

Autumn 1975

P eople got killed, kidnapped, injured, or maimed. Massacres took place. Many lost their houses or their livelihoods. During the first year of the civil war, each Lebanese community, along sectarian lines, armed themselves in various degrees in order to defend their patch and people against any sort of aggression. But normal life, too, went on in Beirut. Marriages took place and babies were born. When there was a lull in the fighting, ordinary people came out of hiding. They went shopping for food and stocked up even if the food they found was not the sort they usually cared for. There were shortages of certain foodstuffs, but it didn't matter what was available as long as it was not quickly perishable. Citizens had to ensure they had enough for when the shelling started again. They also bought clothing, furniture, household equipment, and cars, and hoped life would get back to normal.

The traffic became congested as usual, and shared 'sér-vice' taxis operated on routes that were temporarily considered safe, that is, anywhere other than the downtown areas where the fighters were king. The chic ladies went to their favourite hairdresser, the sick paid the overdue visit to their physician, and relatives visited each other to celebrate that they were still alive. Even though schools and universities remained closed during that first year of fighting, youngsters found ways to entertain themselves with music, reading, TV, parties held locally, or sports in their locales. Some, both males and females, were trained on the use of simple firearms or received instruction on first aid techniques within their communities.

On one occasion when the fighting had ceased for a few days, Tony, Michel and Nora decided to go and investigate the area nearest to the Green Line that was accessible on foot from their neighbourhoods. Unaware of the dangers, they had the natural curiosity of young people of their age and wanted to see the demarcation line between East and West Beirut in that particular area for themselves. The closer they got to the Green Line, the fewer people they saw on the streets. As they moved closer, they felt the unease in people – why did the handful of people they saw on the street walk so quickly on the right pavement and not on the left one? They soon discovered the reason. They took a couple of steps forward and noticed that the buildings on the left side of the street were like blocks of gruyere cheese, riddled with bullet holes. And then they spotted the large opening between two corner buildings. The expanse between them was blocked with three giant metal cargo containers, placed on top of each other. 'Get back! Get back! Snipers! What are you doing here?' An old man was yelling and gesturing to them as he walked towards them. The old man must have been a resident of the locale who probably still lived there and had nowhere else to go. But Tony, Michel, and Nora didn't stop to inquire. They turned around and hastily left the area, vowing never to repeat the experience.

On another occasion, ten days of heavy shelling had holed up Tony and Michel in the basement, a make-shift bomb shelter, of their modern, high-rise apartment block. Before they shifted to the basement with all the other neighbours of the building, Tony called Nora to see how she was doing. She said she and her family were going to the basement of the school attached to the Armenian Church and club, a five-minute walk away. She said there were no bomb shelters in the vicinity and her family had decided this was the safest place to be. When the intense shelling came to an end, Tony attempted to call Nora again, but the telephone lines were dead. He had to make sure she was alright. The best thing to do, he thought, was to drive to her location. Michel came along. They both told their parents where they were going and not to worry if they didn't come back in the evening in case the shelling started again. It took Tony five minutes to get to Nora's location. She was certainly overjoyed to see them both.

"My parents think it's too soon to get back to the apartment," she said. And they were right. An hour after Tony and Michel got to the school basement, the shelling started again. So now they were stuck and had to spend the night there.

The Armenian school basement was in fact the school's very large gym. There were at least 40 or 50 families from the area who had sought shelter there. They'd been there for ten days, some even longer. At the start of the hostilities, an Armenian oriental carpet dealer had moved his inventory from a downtown area and stored hundreds of carpets and rugs in that school gym. The piles of rugs were a God-sent to all those families. They used some of the carpets as base mattresses and placed their beddings on top of them. Everyone had brought their water and food supplies with them. But locked up in one location, the days seemed too long. To keep busy, mothers took turns to cook on the few portable gas camping-cookers that were available; they made endless rounds of coffee for everyone, and occasionally read each other's coffee grounds. Fathers played backgammon and chain-smoked. Youngsters played cards or scrabble to pass the time. The very young ran around in circles in the empty areas of the gym making a huge racket, but no one had the heart to chide them.

That night the shelling was so intense that no one could sleep. Tony, Michel, and Nora marked the intensity of the shelling. A rocket fell roughly every two minutes. One could hear a rocket's whistling sound and then its loud bang.

"May God help us!" an older woman kept on repeating.

"I hope my Fiat is still there tomorrow morning," said Tony, rolling his eyes.

With sunrise the shelling had stopped. The three of them, like all the others in the gym, came out of hiding to assess the damage done to their surroundings. The Fiat was still intact but was entirely covered in a fine layer of white dust. A little further down the road there was debris from a nearby building. It was the remains of a balcony that had collapsed by a direct rocket hit. On the other side of the street, a tall building had taken a bad hit. Its side had a gaping hole.

"Good news, everyone! There's some kind of an agreement between the warring factions! A truce of sorts. I just heard it on the radio," shouted someone.

"At last! We can now go home," someone else said.

It was during the ensuing ceasefire and when telephone lines were back that Tony, Michel and Nora planned to cross the Green Line and visit their friends on the other side of Beirut. They had not seen Waleed, Carole, and Sana for over a month. It was possible to see Ramzi there, too. Ramzi had called Tony a few days earlier and told him that his parents and younger sisters wished to remain in their village near Byblos, but that he'd taken the decision to live with his uncle in the southern suburbs of Beirut. He said he couldn't stay away from Sana. It would be easier to see her if he had easy access to West Beirut. His parents hadn't objected to his decision to move. They even welcomed it. They were of the opinion that although Ramzi was a Shiite and Shiites so far had not taken sides in the conflict, they feared for him. After all, he was still a Muslim living in a Christian-dominated area.

The morning the three of them crossed the Green Line through the Tabaris Highway to Spears Street, all was quiet on the front. There were no road blocks in sight. The beginning of the short highway was not a problem.

The danger began at a specific point on the highway which could be seen by snipers from either camp. The high walls of the highway protected them from the left, but they were sitting ducks from the right. The secret of avoiding snipers was to accelerate at that precise location. And that's exactly what Tony did. Right before reaching it, Tony put his foot down. He concentrated on the road ahead, not looking right or left. His tiny Fiat's speed soon reached its maximum of 120 km. For a tiny car, its Italian engine made a lot of noise like a supped-up rally car. With the car moving so fast, Michel fell on the seat at the back. Nora, sitting in the front seat, next to Tony, was holding the handle of the door, terrified. In two minutes flat they were on the other side of the Green Line. They were safe and sound.

They directly headed towards Waleed's apartment in the Clemenceau area. But, all through their day in West Beirut, Nora kept reminding Michel and Tony that they had to repeat the horrible experience when going back to East Beirut.

"So happy to see you guys! We've been waiting for you impatiently," said Waleed.

"We missed you so much," Carole said and gave each one of them a hug and kisses on the cheeks.

Ramzi and Sana were already there and greeted them with enthusiasm.

"Can't believe you're here," Sana said.

"I've been dreaming of this moment," added Ramzi. "Any trouble on the way? Anyone stopped you?"

"No. All was fine. In any case, if any of the militia stopped us, they could see I'm Armenian, Michel is Greek Catholic, and Tony's Greek Orthodox – we represent the neutrals in the conflict," said Nora.

"How long is this shitty conflict going to last?" Waleed butted in.

"No one knows. We have to live for the day," Ramzi responded. "Let's go to Hamra!"

Hamra's eateries, cafés, and shops were all open. It was hard to believe that a short distance away the militias were shooting at each other, killing each other, and destroying all the recently built waterfront five-star hotels.

But the seven of them didn't want to think about all those things. They wanted to enjoy each other's company and have a good time whilst they could. Their type of friendship was a new phenomenon in a divided country. While other friendships had ended because of the geographical division of the city along sectarian lines, every single one of the seven friends had realized that their friendship had strengthened with the civil war. They were compelled to seek each other even if it meant putting themselves in danger. Despite their differences, they wholeheartedly reached out for each other and were willing to fight against the odds to preserve their camaraderie. On that day, they laughed and joked and, over coffee, also recounted the terrifying moments they had lived through the shelling. West Beirut had had its share of the shelling as much as East Beirut. They finally ended up having a copious meal of marinated chicken kebabs and other assorted delicacies that lasted for over three hours.

"Hey, we have to do this whenever we can. We can't let those bastards rule our lives," said Waleed when it was time for Tony, Michel, and Nora to head back to East Beirut.

"That's right," said Ramzi.

"Call one of us when you're back there if the lines are okay," Carole said.

"May God be with you," said Sana in a barely audible voice, looking concerned.

It was almost the evening when they headed back, but there was still light. Tony readied himself to accelerate again even before they reached the point where they could be spotted by the snipers. Michel and Nora held their breaths and not a single word came out of either of them.

"Here we go!"

Tony revved the car and away they went. The car sped again at its maximum speed. A few minutes later, they were out of sight of the snipers. Tony began slowing the car down.

"We made it!"

As soon as Michel said those words, they heard the whistling sound of an RPG rocket. And a few seconds later, another, and then another, and another. All three could hear the thunderous explosions afterwards. Boom! Boom! Boom! They were still on the highway.

"Don't worry, we've only got a few hundred metres and we'll exit the highway," Tony said.

And then a rocket exploded right in front of them, in mid-air. They could see the smoke ahead and the debris falling on the road.

"Accelerate! Accelerate!" Nora was shouting now. She immediately felt her heart beating very fast and her knees shaking out of fear.

Tony drove as fast as he could and then swerved to the right to get off the highway and into Ashrafieh. Just at that very moment he noticed that another car, a few metres ahead of his, was also getting off the highway and swerving to the right, but Tony couldn't decrease his speed. As he swerved to the right, he clipped the other car's side corner. But he didn't care and he didn't have the intention of stopping. He overtook the other car. The other car's driver looked at him for a split of a second and made the same decision. This was no time to stop for anything. It was raining rockets!

"Are you two alright?"

"Yes, yes, carry on," shouted Michel.

"I'll take you home, Nora," Tony said and kept his foot on the accelerator.

"Call me when you reach home," she said five minutes later as she was leaving the car. The rockets still kept on coming.

Tony did call her, the minute he and Michel got home. She was relieved to hear his voice even though she had to answer it sitting on the floor. The rockets rained for another hour before they stopped.

She called Tony later.

"I don't know if any of us will survive all this," she told him.

"We made it, didn't we?"

"We sure did, Tony. But to tell you the truth, I was terrified and my knees were shaking – even when I got home."

"It's a perfectly normal reaction. I myself felt my heart beating ever so fast and I prayed I still had the strength to continue driving," he said.

"Every time a rocket fell, we'd all duck here at home. My mother was beseeching the Creator. She didn't stop calling out to the Lord. I finally gave up ducking and sat on the floor until the rockets stopped. This was an unexpected attack of such force that no one had time to even make it to a shelter."

"It was, and now it's all quiet," Tony said and then added, "but the adrenalin was flowing when we were in the car. It was exciting. Admit it."

"I won't lie to you. Yes, coming face-to-face with danger is exhilarating, I'll admit it. But can we do this sort of thing again? It's really too dangerous," Nora said, concerned.

"Wasn't it great seeing our friends? Wasn't it fantastic all of us being together? I'd do it again."

"Me too," she said and surprised herself as she was saying it.

"Listen, Tony, don't ever tell my parents about the rocket that exploded right in front of us. In truth, it could have landed on the car instead of exploding in the air. The three of us would be dead now – and in pieces. I haven't told them. They'd go crazy and would never allow me to go in your car ever again."

"Alright, promise. What do you think of my second-hand car now? The Fiat performed pretty well today considering it's an old teeny-weeny little thing. It made me proud."

"I love it! Was there much damage?"

"No. It's just a little dent. I'll have it fixed as soon as possible."

"Thanks, Tony for getting me back home safe and sound. We'll have to call our friends to let them know we're safe."

"I'll do that as soon as we hang up."

"Is Michel alright?"

"Yes, he's fine. No worries. I'm taking good care of him," Tony laughed and then added, "I'll come around and see you when I can."

"I hope very soon," she said, "I'll be waiting."

CHAPTER 6
MICHEL

"What the fuck are you doing in the bathroom? You've been in there for over 20 minutes."

"Alright, alright, I'm coming out."

Michel's older, half-brother, Fady, started banging on the bathroom door now.

"You're not a girl. You don't need to spend so much time in there," he said in a sarcastic tone and waited for Michel's response that never came.

"If you don't come out right this very minute, I'll break down the door."

Michel opened the door and didn't look at Fady. The twerp always displayed the face of someone who was full of guilt. That's what Fady thought anyway. The small creature filled him with hate and disgust.

"How many times do I have to tell you not to monopolize the bathroom?"

Michel ignored him and, lowering his eyes, walked past him and headed towards his bedroom.

"You're a real shit, you know that? I'd curse your mother right now if she weren't married to my father."

"I'll kill you if you ever say anything about my mother, you hear?" shouted Michel. This was one of the few times he had answered Fady back and he knew what was coming.

"I'll show you who's boss round here," Fady said and like an enraged bull attacked him. He was much bigger than Michel and so much unlike him. He was tall and burly. He had a good bit of muscle built around his frame. He had trained as a wrestler in the past.

Fady pushed Michel and smacked him on the cheeks, shoulders, and sides as he began screaming his head off.

"You're a filthy dog. You think you can challenge me because you've turned 18? Huh? You think you're a hero? Huh? Have you seen the way you walk? You effeminate cunt," he shouted and continued to hit him hard until their father, hearing the commotion, intervened.

"My sons, my sons, for the love of God, please stop this," he said and pulled Fady away from Michel.

This was Michel's home life. Fady had bullied him ever since he was a small child. He hated Fady as much as Fady hated him. If it weren't for his mother, who protected him when he was younger, he was certain Fady would have killed him.

Things got really difficult when he went into puberty. He must have been around 13 when he got a right old beating from Fady. At that stage, his mother was no longer by his side at all times like she'd been when he was younger. She could no longer protect him. It was over a shirt that he'd bought for himself using his pocket money. The shirt was a fashionable number with large flowers in bright colours. He wore it to go out and that's when Fady caught sight of him. He mocked him. He said only a woman would wear such a pattern and stopped him from going out. Michel refused to obey him. Fady, enraged, got up from his seat and gave him blows on his face and all over his body. Not only that, but he forced him to remove the shirt and tore it to pieces.

The next day, his mother took him to the doctor. One side of his face was badly swollen and he had bruises all over. Alone together in his bedroom upon their return, his mother applied the cream that the doctor had prescribed. And then she whispered.

"Micho, my darling Micho, listen to me. I'm as upset as you are about what happened, but please, don't ever contradict Fady again and always get out of his way. Please, Micho, I'm begging you."

Michel was livid about what had transpired, but he also felt sorry for himself. This bullying and beating could go on no more. He was on the verge of a nervous breakdown and couldn't help thinking about committing suicide. They'd all be better off without him, he thought. He considered the different ways he could do it for a week but couldn't settle on one method. Ten days later, he had decided to forget about committing suicide. It wasn't an easy decision to take. First, it was against his religion. And second, it would mean he had lost and Fady would have won. From that day forward, things were going to change, he thought. He asked his mother to have a lock system put on his bedroom door. At least Fady would not have access to it and would not be able to rummage through his belongings like he sometimes did. His mother complied and with the help of his father the matter was settled. After school, he tried to do his homework at a friend's house, or if that was not possible, in the public park nearby just to avoid coming across Fady at home. He went home at suppertime and felt secure in the presence of his mother and father. As soon as he finished his supper, he locked himself in his bedroom, only occasionally opening it if his mother wanted to talk to him about something.

But things were not that simple. He was deprived of watching TV with his parents because Fady did. He bought a turn-table and placed it on his work desk, which he no longer used. But whenever he played music, Fady banged on his door and shouted obscenities, complaining that the music was too loud. In other words, there was no way of avoiding Fady altogether. He was depressed most of the time and felt like a prisoner in his own home. That is, until the day he met Tony.

They were both 14 when Tony and his family moved into the building. They were a breath of fresh air for Michel. When he first befriended Tony, he could tell Tony was going to be his saviour. Not only did they have the same taste in music and liked football, but also their personalities matched. Tony was always calm and considerate. He was good-natured and didn't express anger. He accepted Michel as he was and treated him as an equal. They became good friends in a matter of weeks. Michel spent most of his time in Tony's apartment. His family was so different to his. There was an atmosphere of love and affection that he so much yearned for in his own home. If only Fady were not there. Michel was certain his presence influenced the behaviour of his parents. Fady's presence poisoned the air in his home.

When he came back from school in the afternoon, he went directly to Tony's. It didn't matter if Tony was there or not. Tony's mum always greeted him as if he were a member of the family. He'd sit at their dining table and do his homework until Tony arrived. Tony's two older sisters showered him with love. The older of the two served him cookies and tea or coffee at tea time and sometimes helped him with his math homework. The younger one, who was the sweetest of girls, gave him a kiss on the cheek if she was around and asked for his opinion regarding her sartorial choices before getting dressed to go out. Tony's father was much younger than his own father, with whom Michel had not much in common. Tony's father was more like a friend to both Tony and him. Whenever there was an important football match, he'd go with them. If Michel wanted advice about something, he'd go to Tony's father not his.

Tony's interest in girls manifested itself a little after they became close friends. That following summer, he was attracted to a girl who lived two blocks away. He dragged Michel along and they walked up and down the girl's street until she eventually appeared on her balcony on the first floor. Tony wanted to make sure she'd seen him. He didn't stop walking but looked up and gave her a smile. This he did for a whole week. At the end of the week, the girl finally smiled back at him. The following week, Michel asked him if they were walking to the girl's street again.

"No, no. Not this week," Tony said.

"But why? Aren't you interested in her anymore?"

"Romance technique, my friend. You'll see what will happen. Not this week. We'll go there next week."

Michel could not really comprehend the game Tony was playing until they went to the girl's street the following week. She was on her balcony when she spotted the two of them walking up the street towards her building. By the time they got there, she was already downstairs at the entrance of her building.

"I'm going to the public garden. Do you want to come along?" she asked.

Tony chatted with the girl all afternoon in the park while Michel hung around like a bad smell, sitting on another bench. When they said goodbye to the girl, Tony said they'd arranged to go out to the cinema together and that she'll bring her friend along.

"What?"

"You're going on a blind date. Now don't complain. I got you a girl, too," Tony said.

Michel's blind date turned out to be the girl's cousin. She was a petite girl who wore glasses but was quite attractive nevertheless. The foursome went to the cinema twice. The moment the lights went out, Tony took the initiative and held his girl's hand all through the film. Michel saw this with the corner of his eye but couldn't bring himself to do the same with his date. A couple of weeks later, they were invited to the birthday party of Michel's blind date girl.

"What kind of present should I be buying her?"

"Well, there are several possibilities," Tony said.

"Best thing is to buy her a bottle of perfume. Calèche by Hérmès. Classic – every woman or girl likes it," Tony's younger sister said overhearing their conversation.

The birthday girl, who welcomed them to the party without her glasses, loved her present. She had invited at least 30 other teenagers and had created a dance floor by moving her parents' furniture out of the living room. Once the cake was cut, everyone began to dance. Soon a slow, romantic song was playing and the lights were dimmed. Michel held the birthday girl in his arms and danced with her for the rest of the evening. At one point, she squeezed his arm and then looking into his eyes planted a kiss on his cheek. But something stopped him. Michel could not kiss her back.

"What do you mean by not kissing her back?! You should have seen yourself. You danced like a stick. A stick without emotions that could break at any moment. What's wrong with you, Michel?" said Tony the next day.

"I don't know," he replied.

The birthday girl never called Michel again. Tony, who had kissed his girl once at the end of the party, went out with her a couple more times, but by the end of the summer, he was infatuated with some other girl he'd met at the beach and he didn't see her again.

When winter came and both spent a lot of time together indoors in Tony's apartment, Tony found a pile of old Playboy magazine issues hidden under his parents' bed. It was a day when every member of Tony's family was absent from the apartment. Tony immediately showed them to Michel.

"Wow! Look at those pair of tits!" he said, all excited. "I tell you what. I'm going to 'borrow' two issues every time. I'll make use of one and I'll give you the other. I'll replace them and get two others every time. My father won't even notice they're missing."

Michel 'borrowed' the magazines from Tony but was incapable of making use of them in his bedroom. He thought there was something not right about his emotions. He felt attracted to men in pictures, not women. There was an older guy who lived down the street that he felt attracted to whenever he saw him. Every time he was alone in his room, he obsessed about it. He couldn't understand these feelings. He struggled with them but did not tell Tony.

When they were sixteen, Tony and Michel had already met Nora, Carole, Sana, Waleed, and Ramzi, but usually went to a football match on their own. Tony's father was not with them on this occasion. There they met a group of four guys from the neighbourhood football club, who were eighteen or nineteen, and joined them. After the match, the boys proposed they go to a brothel.

"We have to go," whispered Tony to Michel. "Can't say no to them. And this is our chance – this is the real deal."

Michel shrugged and went along.

A woman, with bleached blond hair and mini skirt, who was past her prime, greeted them with a big smile at the brothel.

"All six of you? Payment upfront, boys. You take turns – you understand? Room 5," she said and pointed towards the room at the end of a wide corridor.

The first one who went in came out of the room five minutes later and said, "Unbelievable! This woman knows exactly how to manipulate your package. Irresistible!"

The guys pushed Tony to go in next. A skinny woman in an open-front kimono was waiting for her next customer. She was dark – dark hair, dark skin, thick dark eyebrows, and he could spot one of her dark nipples. She could be of gypsy origin or maybe she's Egyptian, he thought. 'Come baby, come habibi', she said with a man-like voice and sucked on her cigarette. He took a few steps forward. He stared at her long, dead face for a while, hesitating to move any further. He suddenly felt nauseous. He took a few steps back. 'Tsk…suit yourself', she said, knowing he would leave. 'Send the next one in…'

"Hey, you were dead quick," said the next guy and went in.

"You want to go in after him?" Tony asked Michel.

"No. Tony, I want to leave. It's not for me," Michel said.

"Let's go then."

They left the brothel without saying goodbye to the other guys. They just slipped out quietly.

"So how was it in there?" asked Michel.

"Terrible. I couldn't do it. The minute I set foot in that room I knew I'd made a mistake. I cringed at the thought. The thought of having her touch me and she's touched hundreds. And I felt disgusted – not with her but with myself."

In his locked room that night, Michel thought of the man who lived down the road. He had been attracted to this man ever since he went into puberty without knowing the exact reason. And then he thought of the young man he had met a few weeks ago. He guessed he was probably in his early 20's. He worked at the bookshop next to his school. The young man had spoken to him – not as much as in words but with his eyes. Recently when he went in there, he was looking through some foreign magazines, displayed at the far corner shelf, when he realized the young man was standing next to him. There was no one else in the bookshop. He couldn't be certain if the young man touched his finger on the magazine that he was holding on purpose or accidentally, but when he looked up, the young man had an affectionate look in his eyes. His lips were full, alluring, inviting him to kiss them. But someone came in and he left the bookshop swiftly.

He had constantly thought about what had happened for days and found himself wishing he could see that young man again and figure out a way of talking to him. A few days earlier, he had finally drummed up the courage to go to the bookshop again. He made a beeline for the foreign magazines as per his usual, too embarrassed to immediately address the young man, who stood behind the cash register. He could never have imagined what happened next. He sensed the young man walking towards him. He stood next to Michel like the previous time but didn't look into his eyes. He then gave him a little piece of paper as if he had prepared it in advance in case Michel turned up at the bookshop again. 'I like you and want to get to know you. Would you go out with me?' Michel looked at those unexpected words for a while and then he scribbled with no hesitation 'Yes. I'll call you tomorrow and we can set a date' on the paper and gave it back to the young man before leaving the bookshop. All was now clear to him. But he knew he had to tell Tony. Would he end their friendship? He was his best friend. He felt compelled to open up to him.

The next day, he went to Tony's as usual. Tony's mum was busy cooking in the kitchen and his sisters were out. Tony arrived from school a half hour later and took his usual seat at the dining table.

"Tony, I've got something important to tell you." he said, lowering his voice. "I don't know how to begin. It's complicated. It's been eating away at me for the last two years."

"Come on buddy! Out with it. I'm no stranger."

"I'll understand if you don't want to see me again after what I've told you. It's difficult."

"What's happening, Michel? Look – I forgive you – whatever you've done. We're best friends, remember? Say it and relieve me!"

"I'm attracted to men – not women," he blurted out.

There was a long pause.

"Are you sure? You were looking at all the girls at the beach club – same as me, telling me how sexy they were. You have the habit of shouting 'Hey lovely girl!' whenever we're in a car when you see an attractive young girl walking down the street."

"I wasn't pretending, Tony. I was trying very hard to act normal, like you. But I was deluding myself. I now know it's not the real me. Do you understand that?"

"I'm trying to. I really need to process this. I mean, you've dropped a real bombshell here. And I don't know what to say to you."

Their conversation was interrupted by the arrival of Tony's two sisters. Michel participated in the casual conversation and left for home earlier than his usual time. He couldn't sleep until the small hours of the morning thinking about how Tony would react next time they met. If he lost Tony's friendship, it would mean the end of the world for him.

When he returned from school the next day, he didn't go up to Tony's apartment. He hung around the entrance of the building until Tony came back from school.

"What are you doing here? Why aren't you upstairs?" Tony inquired.

"I was waiting for you."

"Michel, it's not easy for me to be in your mind and body. All I know is we're best friends. You are who you are and I am who I am. That's all," Tony said in a firm tone and then added, "Unless you're attracted to me. If that's the case, you're out of my life," he said and laughed.

"You know very well I'm not. You're more than my best friend. You're my brother."

"And you don't have to tell me to keep this from everyone else. Your secret is safe with me."

"I know." Michel paused for a moment. "But I don't mind you telling Nora. She's the only one who'll understand."

"Okay. Let's go upstairs."

CHAPTER 7

THE WHITE COFFIN

Winter 1976

"I don't get it. How can you let Fady beat you up? You're not a child anymore. You're almost 19, Michel. His behaviour is really unacceptable. We need to do something, teach him a lesson, frighten him somehow," said Tony with an indignant tone.

"Don't get too worked up, my friend. Put your mind at ease. I won't have to see Fady for much longer. He's talking about getting engaged to that peroxide-blonde girlfriend of his next week and they plan to marry within the year, meaning he will move out of the house. And..."

"That's the best news I've heard in a long time! And what?"

"I've been called to do my military service with the Lebanese Army. The papers arrived this morning," Michel said.

"What? How come I wasn't called?"

"You, Ramzi and Waleed will not be called. You're the only male sons in your families. The army won't take you."

"Shit! Fady's done it again. I wish you didn't have a half-brother," Tony said, shaking his head.

"Honestly, I don't mind going. It's only for a short while. It'll be over in no time and I don't mind not sleeping in my house until Fady is out of there. In any case, the Lebanese Army hasn't taken sides in the civil war. It'll be the patriotic thing to do," Michel said with conviction.

"Guess you're right, but I shall miss you," Tony said.

"Hey, it's only for a short time and you have Nora to keep you company."

Michel, Nora and Tony had a calm Christmas and New Year that allowed them to see each other before Michel left to do his military service. And although the fighting had subsided over the holiday period, Waleed, Carole, Ramzi and Sana were unable to cross the Green Line because of heavy sniper activity. Michel reported to his assigned barracks in Beirut in early January. The day he left, Nora and Tony went to his house for the first time ever to say goodbye to him. His mother was distraught. She had erected a 'shrine' in one corner of the living room, next to the colourful Christmas tree. A large statue of the Virgin Mary sat on a solid wooden table. The Virgin was surrounded with flowers and was lit up even though it was morning and the sun rays penetrated the living room.

"O Virgin, O Virgin, please protect my Micho," Michel's mother repeated like a mantra, looking at the statue every so often.

"Mum, stop worrying," Michel said and carried on his conversation with Tony and Nora.

When it was time for him to leave, Tony and Nora hugged him tightly and so did his mum and dad. Fady was nowhere to be seen. And his mother multiplied her prayers.

"May you be the one to bury me – my only son! O Virgin, O Jesus, protect my Micho!"

Everyone knew that the proud Lebanese Army had so far remained impartial in the civil strife. No one expected anyone to rip it into sectarian pieces so easily. Two days after the Karantina massacre, on January 21, 1976, First Lieutenant Ahmad Al-Khatib, gave the Lebanese Army its first blow. Al-Khatib, a Sunni Muslim, led a rebellion with a group of soldiers. It was widely believed he was backed by the Palestinian Command and financed by Libya. His movement began taking over Lebanese Army barracks one by one.

The Al-Khatib rebellion was unsuccessful though. The Lebanese Army was able to contain the rebellion within a few days, but it was too late for Michel. His barracks was the first one to be attacked by Al-Khatib's supporters. They killed all the Christians who were stationed in the barracks, which was located in the Beirut area. Michel and an Armenian, who was also doing his military service, were on guard duty the night of the rebellion. Both were shot in the back.

News of the murder of Michel reached his family and Tony and Nora a few days later, once the Lebanese Army took back control of all the barracks that were attacked and taken by the rebels.

"No, No, No!!!" Nora shouted when Tony gave her the bad news. She cried uncontrollably for several hours afterwards. Tony tried to comfort her, but he was crying inside, too.

"We need to go and see his mum," Tony said eventually. "I think the funeral is scheduled to take place tomorrow."

"What's going to become of us?" Nora said and blew her nose. "He's the first one of us seven to go. And to think he was shot in the back. He was innocent. He had nothing to do with any of this. A cowardly, treacherous act. I'm terrified, Tony. But more than that, I can't believe he's gone. It's incomprehensible – absurd!"

"I've lost my dearest friend, Nora, and I don't know if I can ever get over it," Tony said and could no longer hold back his tears. His tears flowed. His earnest effort not to cry in front of Nora had disappeared. He couldn't remember the last time he had cried like that. He closed his eyes and saw Michel's face. He was smiling at him like he did the last time they saw each other. They had said goodbye before Michel left for the army barracks in a waiting taxi. But before he got in, he'd turned around, and had innocently smiled at Tony one more time. That was the last image of Michel and Tony would cherish it for the rest of his life.

"We've got to get out of here," Nora broke the heavy silence and wiped the tear drops from Tony's face.

<hr>

We shot him against the light
and allowed hatred to rise like baked bread
from "Nothing but a Man" by Nadia Tueni (trans. from the
French by the author)

"A Lebanese Army officer and a group of soldiers will deliver the casket to the church tomorrow. They told me that the casket must not be opened and will be covered with the Lebanese flag," said Fady to his father.

Michel's mother, who was sitting next to her husband, opened her swollen eyelids for the first time in hours.

"I have ordered a white coffin. He was only a child, barely 19. And the animals who slaughtered my son will burn in hell. But we will celebrate my son's wedding with music, pomp and ceremony like it is our custom when someone is taken at such a young age, not his funeral," she said calmly but defiantly. She then turned to her husband for support.

"You can't do that. The army people won't have it. They will deliver his body in a brown, standard issue army coffin and the funeral will take place as per the army's instructions. And that's that!" Fady said, raising his voice.

"Over my dead body," Michel's mother retorted. "Enough is enough. I want my son to have a funeral to my own liking and according to our traditions. You hurt him enough when he was alive. You're not going to hurt him in death. You call the army people and tell them that the casket has to be delivered to Michel's home and you have to do it right now," Michel's mother ordered.

Fady opened his mouth to object. But his father stopped him.

"Fady, my son, for once do as you're told. Always remember that Michel was my son, too. And, I, your father, wants Michel's funeral to be exactly the way his mother wishes it," he said in a very firm tone – a tone he'd never used before.

And for once, Fady complied with his father's wishes. He negotiated with the army to have Michel's casket delivered to the house and a compromise was reached. Michel would have a traditional funeral, but the coffin would be shut once it entered the church. It would then be covered with the Lebanese flag.

Tony and Nora were already at Michel's house when the casket was delivered the next day. The apartment was full of close relatives and friends. Everyone could feel Michel's mother's grief. The grief was contagious and stifling.

"Open the casket. I want to make sure it's him," she ordered.

The casket lid was removed. Michel's child-like face appeared with a bandaged head and his small body seemed to have shrunk and looked even smaller. He was like a tiny cherub. His mother let out a shrill wail and touched his face and then kissed it. Everyone present was crying.

"Micho, my son! Wake up! We're going to celebrate your wedding!"

She let out another shrill wail, and another, and another, until she turned ash grey and fainted. Nora and other women came to her rescue and tried to revive her, slapping her cheeks and sprinkling cologne water on her face.

Michel's father, visibly shaken by seeing his dead son, got a hold of himself, and as the head of the household, ordered for the casket to be taken to the other room where the white coffin lay.

"Let's put him in the white coffin," said Fady.

Tony and a few others were there to help. As soon as Tony touched Michel's dead body, he was overwhelmed by emotions and lost his strength to lift it.

"Step aside," Fady said and lifted the upper part of the body with all his strength. Others lifted the legs and transferred Michel's body to the white coffin.

And then they heard the music. It was the traditional funerary group of musicians, dressed in military-type attire. They were playing their brass instruments and drum to their highest volume in front of the building.

"It's time to go," Michel's father said.

The sad procession started from Michel's house to the church which was about 400 metres away. It was the first of such processions that Nora had seen. The tradition was alien to her community's traditions. She found Tony and they followed the procession.

The musicians at the forefront announced the coming of the funerary procession. They were followed by the bearers of the coffin lid. They danced the lid to the tune of the music in the hope of waking up the dead. The coffin lid bearers were followed by the poll bearers. They swung Michel's lifeless body, sleeping in the white coffin, right to left and left to right. And then up and down. Wasn't this his 'wedding'? He should wake up!

People in the neighbourhood were out on their balconies watching the procession. Some had come out on the streets and a few could be heard shouting hate slogans against Muslims. Women at the top of the procession were propping Michel's mother. She didn't have the strength to carry herself. Other women were crying and wailing like traditional wailers. The men followed the women in silence.

When the funerary procession reached the church, the Lebanese Army officer and soldiers were waiting at the door. And as it was agreed, they took charge of the coffin. They covered it with the lid and draped the Lebanese flag on the white coffin and carried it inside.

Neither Nora nor Tony could remember what was said by the priest. Both were crying all through the funeral mass. In the end, all they could focus on was Michel's mother who touched the coffin one last time before they took it to the cemetery. She had exhausted all her tears. She was no longer herself. Her eyes were like unmoving glass balls and her white, wax-like face appeared as if she was in a trance. She was mumbling things that were incomprehensible except something that she repeated over and over again.

"You left me to bury you. Wake up my handsome groom."

The next months were terribly sad for Tony and Nora. They couldn't come to terms with Michel's death. It was the same at Tony's where neither his mother nor his sisters could stop mentioning Michel as, certainly, he was considered part of their family, too. The few times Nora and Tony could meet up with Waleed, Carole, Ramzi, and Sana the get-togethers were punctuated by reminiscing about their time with Michel.

"He was the best of us lot," Nora said at their last meeting.

"He was innocence personified," said Waleed.

"Only the good die young," said Sana and began to cry and made Carole weep to such an extent that she had to excuse herself and left the room.

None of them could reconcile with the fact that they were no longer seven in the group. It was as if Michel's death was the all-encompassing tragedy hovering over their existence and foreboding tragedies yet to come.

And Michel wasn't the only victim. They all knew this – so many people were still getting killed – some by snipers, others by stray bullets, massacres, car bombs, rockets and shrapnel – and the atrocities didn't stop.

"I have terrible news to give you," Tony said to Nora one afternoon when he came over for a visit.

"Not again! Not another bad news. What's happened now?"

"Michel's family has already forgotten about him. For God's sake, his funeral was only four months ago and his mother has already forgotten about him."

"What do you mean, Tony? You can't be serious."

"I'm telling you they're acting as if he never existed. What a tragedy. I will always cherish his memory. He was my best friend and I didn't care if he was gay. But his mother..."

"Tony, please elaborate," said Nora alarmed.

"Michel's mother is pregnant. She told my mum yesterday. She's 42. Can you believe it?"

"I see," said Nora and paused for a while.

"Well, I'm right, am I not? How can you forget a son who was savagely killed and have the appetite to have another child? I don't get it."

"Tony, please. Don't be so harsh on her. People deal with grief and tragedy in different ways. I think you're taking this the wrong way."

"Am I? It's supposedly a girl. Replacing a son with a daughter. She probably always wanted to have a daughter anyway and not Michel."

"Stop talking nonsense. Michel cannot be replaced. But his mother has all this love in her for Michel. And she has more love to give to another offspring. Do you understand?"

"I'm trying to but it's not easy to comprehend."

"What right have you got to judge the behaviour and actions of Michel's mother? It's not proper," said Nora and held out her hand to Tony. He took it and squeezed it tightly. He then held it against his chest and lowering his eyes in shame, he nodded in agreement.

CHAPTER 8
ABU ALI'S PLACE

Ramzi and Sana had fallen in love despite themselves. It was the first time for both of them and it could not be reversed. At the young age that they were, their world *was* the two of them. And how can you 'un-love' the one you love? Ramzi, who thought of Sana as his future wife and the mother of his children, was confident of his deftness to find a solution to their predicament. He thought long and hard about the means of convincing her family that he was worthy of marrying a Sunni girl. To this end, he had to first and foremost secure a comfortable living for her as was expected in a Middle Eastern society. The moment he graduated from nursing school, he would start saving money even if it meant relocating to Saudi Arabia or to some other Arabian Gulf country where salaries were at least triple those of Lebanon. He was not one to shy away from doing overtime work, if necessary, either. A more important decision he had taken was his willingness to leave his Shiite Islam behind, at the great displeasure of his own family, and become a Sunni himself in order to marry her. And this, he had discussed with Sana at great length with every little detail of his plans for the future.

Sana's love for him was boundless and she believed every word he told her. She admired Ramzi's determination and questioned her worthiness of having his unfailing affection. And although she adored him, she lacked his courage and confidence. She chided herself for being so weak when she thought of her father and how he would react when faced with the prospect of a Shiite son-in-law. From her sisters she'd heard of quite a few Shiite women marrying Sunni men. They'd even mentioned some by name. But a Sunni woman marrying a Shiite man was a rarity. This information had dented her confidence even further and she took every precaution when meeting with Ramzi lest her father found out.

"How's my lovely girl today," said Ramzi.

He hadn't called for a week and Sana was terribly worried although she knew it was because of the intense shelling on both sides of Beirut which had only subsided the day before. She hadn't gone out and hung around the phone in case he called.

"Hi, Carole! I'm fine and I miss you lots," Sana replied. This was the way she talked to him on the phone. Her family knew Carole and she couldn't take chances if her father or anyone else in the family overheard the conversation.

"Can we meet? I'll pick you up from the usual spot, on Bliss Street, in one hour."

"Yes, okay. See you then," she said and hung up.

"Where are you going?" Her mother asked.

"Going to meet Carole in Hamra. We're having dinner together so won't be back before 8," Sana said.

"You be careful. The minute you hear shelling or gun-fire, you must hurry back."

As she left the house, she felt guilty for lying to her mother but she couldn't help it. She had to see Ramzi.

"Shall we go to Abu Ali's Place?" Ramzi asked when she got into his car.

When they met on their own, without their group of friends, Abu Ali's Place was their regular rendezvous venue. It was a non-descript local eatery, tucked away in one of the side-streets of Hamra. From the street, the ground floor of the restaurant looked like a greasy spoon eatery. And, in a certain way, it was. At the entrance, the neon lights of the large refrigerator that displayed meat on kebab skewers made the place look even more unattractive. Ramzi and Sana were not sure if Abu Ali was aware of this. But the minute he'd see them come in, he'd call out the only waiter he'd hired, and they'd be quickly whisked to the mezzanine floor. The mezzanine floor, almost invisible from down-stairs, had a completely different atmosphere to the one downstairs: dimmed lights, dark wood panelling, plush, velvet-covered divan seats and tasteful tablecloths. They'd hardly seen any other patrons in the upstairs dining area when they were there probably because not many people knew of its existence having been put off by the downstairs' shabby décor. The privacy that the place offered them was unmatched elsewhere and they didn't care if the so-called home-made stews on the menu they had to order were too greasy and practically inedible.

"They're here again," said Ramzi, leaning down from the balustrade.

The downstairs patrons were exclusively local taxi drivers and like Abu Ali, Shiite. They ordered their kebabs and hummus. Ramzi and Sana could hear their animated conversations and laughter.

"What are they doing?" asked Sana.

"They're just having a good time. I can see one of them just poured himself a glass of 'arak' and another guy, a glass of whisky. Abu Ali's place is unlicensed. They're hiding the bottles under the table," said Ramzi and laughed.

Sana giggled and then held Ramzi's hand. He took her other hand and kissed it.

"I'm so glad to see you again, Sana. I thought this day would never come."

She touched his cheek affectionately and gave him a kiss on his other cheek. It was at Abu Ali's Place that they had kissed for the first time. They had kissed many times since – at dance parties with their group of friends. A few times, they had the opportunity of going further after gatherings at Waleed's when his parents were away and Waleed had the apartment to himself. On one of these occasions, and after a heavy petting session in Waleed's guest bedroom, they had both decided not to go all the way:

"I know some of our friends and classmates are sleeping with each other, but I want to be a virgin when you marry me," Sana said, expressing the long-held norm in society.

"It's not that Sana. I don't really care if you were a virgin or not on our wedding day. I just want you to know that I respect you and wouldn't want for you to be harmed in any way. We don't know what the future holds for us and until I am sure you're going to be my wife, I won't take any chances," Ramzi said and added, "And hear this – I'll love you 'til the end of time."

"Me too," Sana said and they hugged each other tightly.

Abu Ali's waiter brought them some water, olives, and nuts to nibble on and disappeared.

"Sana, I was so hoping you could meet me today. I've got some good news to give you."

"Go ahead, my love. We certainly need some good news in our lives with all the shelling we've been subjected to," she said.

"We're going to be able to meet each other more often now. I've moved from Byblos to the southern suburbs of Beirut. I'm staying with my uncle."

"Wow! That *is* good news! I so miss our university days. I could see you every day and now we don't know when the nursing school will re-open. If you're in the southern suburbs at least I'll know you won't be far away from me."

"Exactly – I thought I couldn't stay away, stuck in Byblos. I convinced my parents that it was better for me to stay with my uncle in case classes resumed. All the passages through the Green Line are now impassable again. And this way, I can drive to West Beirut with no hassle and meet with you whenever possible," he said and smiled.

"I'm so thrilled!"

"And that's not all the good news. Yesterday I got a job!"

"What?!"

"It's only on a part-time basis but it's something. I was offered a nurse's position at the clinic run by the Shiite religious association in the southern suburbs, an association headed by none other than the Imam himself!"

"Congratulations! But you're not a fully licensed nurse yet."

"I know, but the people running the place don't care. They want to serve the poor population in those neighbourhoods. They're desperate for anyone who knows anything about health care, especially with this damn civil war," Ramzi said and added, "Can you imagine some patients called me Doctor Ramzi this morning? I didn't have the heart to correct them."

Abu Ali's waiter brought them the stew and rice. In order not to seem rude, they each had a couple of mouthfuls and left the rest. All they wanted was to be in each other's presence until it was time for Sana to get home by 8 pm.

⇒╬⇐

"Your father's cousins are coming for a visit this evening. Wear something nice to greet them," Sana's mother said.

"Why? What does that mean?"

"Sana, listen to me. You need to be presentable. Your father said they are interested in asking for your hand for their son, Ahmad."

"Well, I don't want to see them. I told you before I'm not interested in getting married right now. I've got to finish nursing school first," said Sana indignantly.

"Tell that to your father."

"Mom, please talk to him. I can't stand this old-fashioned system of arranged marriages. Please, Mom."

"Alright, I will put it to him as diplomatically as I possibly can. And I don't know how he will react. But in the meantime, you need to make an appearance tonight – to save face."

Sana reluctantly wore her best clothes and participated in the evening. She served baklava and coffee to the guests and took part in the trivial chit-chat. She noticed Ahmad looking at her now and again, checking her out. She really got annoyed and felt like leaving the room but she stopped herself. Only another half hour and they'll be gone she thought. Ahmad was quite a good-looking young man, and in her estimation, not the repulsive type of guy which made women recoil. But in her heart, there was only space for Ramzi.

She was on tender hooks for the next days, not knowing what was going on between her father and the cousins. Then, one morning, her father asked to speak to her privately before heading to work.

"My cousins are keen on asking for your hand for Ahmad. What do you say?" Her father began.

"I don't want to get married before I finish my studies," Sana replied.

"I know, your mother told me. There's no urgency, Sana. Ahmad has to finish his studies, too. I have to respond to them though. If you don't have any objections, how about saying 'yes' to them for now and we'll see about an official engagement at a later date?"

"I don't want an engagement!" Sana burst out crying.

"There's no need to cry, Sana. I won't do anything that you won't agree with."

"I don't want to get married," Sana said and started another round of wailing.

"May God help me and give me strength! Stop crying for God's sake, Sana. This is what I'm going to do. I'm going to tell them that in principle there are no objections but that you need time to get used to the idea, to finish your studies, etc. etc. I'll tell them there won't be anything official for a while and we'll talk about all this in the near future. Does that suit you?"

Sana couldn't think of anything to say. She could not open her heart to her father so she just nodded.

Sana and Ramzi's next meeting, at Abu Ali's Place, was a sad affair. They had just heard of Michel's murder from Tony and Nora. The two hours that they were there was punctuated with a great deal of tears.

"I can't believe Michel is not with us anymore. We weren't even able to attend his funeral. How can such a tragedy befall on us? I'm scared for us, Sana. I'm so fearful that something terrible might happen to us. Sometimes I lie awake at night and have these awful thoughts of us being forcibly separated. I'd go mad if that happens."

It was then that Sana reluctantly recounted the whole incident with her father's cousins and reassured Ramzi that she had the situation under control.

Ramzi was livid. He cursed his luck over and over again.

"It's tormenting," he said. "There's no other solution but to elope. And we have to do it without wasting any more time."

"Ramzi, please, listen to me. Elopement is out of the question. Where would we go? We can't leave the country. We don't have any money. And if we elope, I won't be able to see my parents and siblings again. I will bring shame on my family," said Sana in tears.

Ramzi covered his face with both hands and said nothing for a while.

"I'm sorry, Sana, you're right. Please forgive me but I'm beside myself. I don't know what to do."

Sana held his hand and looked in his eyes, as if beseeching him to find a solution. The whole situation was a nightmare she was hoping to wake up from. She thought of the evening with the cousins and Ahmad for a split of a second. The idea of marrying someone other than Ramzi was so alien to her that she felt sick.

"Okay," Ramzi said in a serious tone and took a deep breath. "Here's what I think. There's no way I can graduate from nursing school as long as universities remain shut and no one knows when they will re-open. So, my hopes of earning money in the Arabian Gulf are dashed. Sana, I have to earn money quickly, here. I can't ask for your hand without having some money behind me. It might take a year or two. Promise that you will stall your family for that period so that you're not forced into marrying your father's cousin's son."

"I promise. But what will you do to earn money?"

"The Shiite religious association has started military training for young men for the purpose of self-defence. You know, all the communities are doing it, right?"

"Right."

"Well, I joined, too. But here's what I was offered on the third day of training. You won't believe this. The guy in charge of the training asked to speak to me after the session. He said that since I was very tall and had the exact physique they were looking for, would I be willing to become one of the bodyguards of the Imam himself. Can you imagine? The Imam! The guy said I had one week to give them an answer and told me that I would be handsomely paid for the job. I think I will go for it. It's our only hope, Sana."

"Are you sure? Isn't it dangerous?"

"I don't think so. The Imam is very popular and highly-thought of by all the different communities in Lebanon as a man of peace. Everyone respects him."

"That's true."

"So, nothing to worry about. Do I have your agreement?"

"Yes, you have my blessing. But still you must be careful, my love," Sana said and tenderly placed her head against Ramzi's shoulder.

"I will. No one is going to stop me from marrying you," Ramzi said, and moving her hair that had fallen on her cheek, he began caressing it.

CHAPTER 9
PARABELLUM 9 MM

End of Spring 1976

N ora contemplated leaving Lebanon. She was utterly convinced that the civil war would not end any time soon. It was five months since Michel's tragic death, and she didn't feel any better. She must be on the verge of having a nervous breakdown, she thought. She knew it would never come to that but that's how she felt. It pained her greatly, but she could not see any future in her country of birth. How about Tony and her friends? Time was passing them by and if things remained as they were, their lives would be destroyed. She had to convince her friends that they had to leave, too.

She recalled a conversation she'd had with Carole and Sana at the beginning of their friendship. It was one that had forged her close relationship with both of them. It had started as a mere girls' talk with Sana complaining about her strict family and saying she was afraid they might find out about Ramzi. Taking her cue from Sana,

Carole had expressed her fear that Waleed was too good to be true and that he would one day cheat on her. Both Sana and Carole had sought a response from Nora, asking her what she would do if she were in their shoes. Nora had responded to Sana by saying, 'You're too self-effacing Sana. You need to be stronger. You need to defend your love. Ramzi, who is totally devoted to you, deserves it'. And to Carole, she'd said, 'If you feel this way, you need to end your relationship with Waleed. You cannot have a true relationship based on lack of self-confidence and mistrust'. Even though reluctantly at the time, both Sana and Carole had admitted she was right. And since then, they'd got into the habit of following her advice and her lead as a matter of course.

What were Nora's and her friends' options? Tony's older sister had already left for Canada. She was allowed in only because she was the fiancée of a Canadian national. The UK, Nora's first choice, was out of the question – the visa rules were very strict. The US was out of bounds, too. Neither she, nor her friends had very close relatives there and university tuition fees were simply unaffordable. Their only chance was to get to France. The French, with close historical ties to the Lebanese, had been very accommodating. Since the start of the civil war in Lebanon, they had facilitated visa procedures and entry to French universities for young Lebanese. One major advantage of continuing her studies in France was the absence of tuition fees. French universities were free even for foreigners.

She put all this to Tony the first chance she had. They discussed it in detail and Tony promptly agreed with her that they had no other choice but to leave Lebanon as soon as possible.

"There's the matter of the language though," he said. "You, Waleed, and I have had all our important subjects in high school and university taught in English. How are we going to adjust to French and at university level?"

"Yes, Carole, Ramzi, and Sana won't have that problem. Well, we'll just have to brush up on our French even if it means losing a few months or even half a year," Nora said and added, "We've got to cross the Green Line soon and find out what the others think about the matter. Maybe we should stay there for at least a week. I've got another idea I wish to pursue. I've heard that Sweden has opened its doors to Lebanese nationals who want to settle there. We need to go to the embassy and obtain more information. But first, I've got to ask permission from my dad."

That evening, when dinner was over, Nora broached the subject with her father. She began with trepidation. She wasn't certain her father would let an 18-year-old girl travel and live in a foreign country on her own. She presented her arguments in the best way she could.

"You seem determined, Nora. And I'm not going to stand in your way. I, too, see that the future, in the current circumstances, does seem bleak for the younger generation. I've lost everything I've worked for all these years and it's too late for me to start all over again. You've got the future ahead of you. I trust you and believe in your ability to achieve great things. I will support you in every way I can. I just want you to remember one thing – your mother and I love you and will always love you," her father said.

"I know," she said and then shyly added, "I promise dad – I will make you proud of me."

⫘⫘

A few days later, Tony and Nora were on their way to West Beirut through the National Museum crossing, the only one that was passable at the time. Although there was a lull in the fighting, snipers were still active on a specific section of the crossing, near the Beirut Hippodrome, and quite a few people had been killed by sniper fire in recent weeks. But like many people who needed to cross, they took their chances. The problem was Tony could not use his car to cross. The roads were blocked for car traffic. They had to undertake the Green Line crossing on foot. And it had to be done by walking through the Hippodrome itself. They thus took a cab to the crossing point in the Green Line. Like them, there were dozens of people waiting to cross over at an opportune moment. Most carried very little with them, but a few were hauling huge suitcases.

After squeezing through concrete barriers, Tony and Nora had to walk a distance of about 200 metres through the Hippodrome track. They followed the dirt path taken by a dozen others ahead of them. At mid-point, people walking ahead of them ducked. This was where snipers had the track in full view. Tony and Nora, fear in their bellies, instinctively ducked, too, and continued moving in that position for the next 50 metres. Tony was carrying Nora's bag in one hand and holding her hand with the other. No one was talking. They finally noticed the guy in front of them stand up and they mimicked him. 'The snipers are asleep this morning', they heard someone say. They nevertheless walked as fast as they could for the remaining distance.

When they got to the concrete barriers on the other side, almost breathless, Waleed and Carole were waiting for them. They had agreed to pick them up.

"Welcome to West Beirut! Let's go!" said Waleed, pointing to his VW Beetle parked a little distance away.

Waleed had barely driven 400 metres when they spotted the checkpoint.

"There was no checkpoint when we came through earlier. What's going on?" said Carole.

"Don't panic. I think it's the Druze militia," said Waleed, and they all witnessed a car being ordered to park on the side of the road and the passengers taken away.

"Don't panic," Waleed repeated. "I can deal with these guys."

"Your IDs," said the Druze militiaman at the checkpoint when it was their turn. He was carrying a machine gun and his features could not be forgotten once one looked at his face. He had a dark, tanned complexion and piercing, large green eyes.

They gave him all four IDs.

"What are you doing with Christians, Druze brother?" he said, turning to Waleed. "Are you returning from the Christian side?" he queried.

"No. I just picked them up from the crossing point. They're my school friends," Waleed said.

"Okay. Pull over. Park your car on the side of the road and leave your keys in. And all of you – come with me."

Waleed did what he was told.

"What are they going to do to us," said Carole, terrified. Nora and Tony kept quiet.

"Calm down! They probably want to steal my car. Tony, Nora, please, don't say a word to them, alright?"

"We're being kidnapped," said Nora.

"For God's sake, just keep quiet! Let me deal with them," said Waleed.

The four of them followed the militiaman. They were taken to a one-storey structure with a rusted iron door, off the main road. Upon entering, they realized it was just a four-walled structure built around an empty expanse. A little hut-like room, with a corrugated iron roof, stood in the middle of it. The militiaman ordered Carole and Nora to stay put. He led Waleed and Tony into the room. Carole and Nora held each other's hands and waited, frightened and horrified. Twenty minutes passed.

"Help us, dear God!" said Carole, "What are they doing to them? They're going to kill them." And she began to cry.

"I'm going to wait two more minutes. If they're not out of that room, I'll bang on the door," Nora said and tried not to think of the worst.

Suddenly, the door of the room opened and Waleed and Tony appeared.

"Let's get out of here. Quick!" said Tony to Carole and Nora.

"What happened in there?" Nora said.

"We'll tell you when we get to the car," Waleed said, "If it's still there."

When they got to the main road, Waleed's car was where they had left it. They got in and drove away as fast as they could.

By the time they got to Waleed's apartment, all was revealed.

They had, in reality, been kidnapped by the Druze militia even if it was only for half an hour. All four were in a state of shock, but they were grateful no harm had come to any of them. The news of their kidnapping, along with that of a dozen other people, was already being reported on the Voice of Lebanon. Nora and Tony knew their parents would be listening to the radio but didn't worry about it since there was no way they'd guess their children were among the occupants of the VW Beetle. Neither of them had told their parents Waleed was picking them up at the crossing. Nevertheless, both Nora and Tony thought they should call their parents to tell them they'd safely crossed to West Beirut.

"What did the Druze militia do to you in that room?" inquired Nora.

"Nothing much," said Tony. "There was what I assume the militiaman's leader sitting at a desk. He asked me who I was and why I was in West Beirut, all the while checking our ID papers."

"He asked me the same question as the militiaman did earlier on and I gave him the same answer," Waleed said. "He then ordered us to empty our pockets. The militiaman who had brought us there went through our belongings. He picked up our wallets and took all the money that was in them."

"So, we were kidnapped to be robbed," Nora said.

"It looks as if the Druze militiamen haven't been paid their wages this week," said Tony sarcastically.

"I definitely need to carry a gun from now on," Waleed said. "Fucking bastards! I won't be humiliated like this again."

"What are you talking about? Stop this nonsense," said Carole, "Just thank God we're all safe and sound."

When over dinner Tony and Nora elaborated on their plan of leaving Lebanon, both Waleed and Carole expressed the same excitement for leaving the country.

"I don't want to stay here anymore. Not after what happened today. How long do you think we need to be ready?" Waleed said.

"Give or take a month or so," Tony replied.

It was agreed that Nora would sleep over at Carole's and Tony at Waleed's during their time in West Beirut. Over the next few days, they contacted some university friends to get detailed information on universities in France, about student accommodation, and about other practicalities. They soon discovered that it would be easy to enrol at a university in Paris, which made them even more eager to leave.

Nora's insistence on going to the Swedish Embassy baffled Tony.

"We've decided to go to Paris. Why do you want to pursue Sweden now?"

"Why not? We might as well since we're in West Beirut and the Swedish Embassy is just around the corner from here. We've got to leave no stones unturned," Nora said.

"I'll wait outside for you. You go in," Tony said when they reached the Swedish Embassy.

Nora returned a good half hour later.

"No dice," she said. "I saw a Swedish consular officer and he said he couldn't give me a visa unless I had all the necessary funds for the duration of my stay and university acceptance letters way ahead of time. When I said won't they take into consideration the situation in Lebanon, he looked me straight in the eye and said, 'Sweden doesn't have an immigration policy.'"

"I told you it was futile to go in there, but you were really stubborn about it," Tony said.

"No, it wasn't futile, Tony. I learned a lesson. When I was waiting to see the consular officer, there was an old Kurdish lady sitting next to me. She had the full Kurdish traditional gear on. She said she was summoned to get her visa to join her son there and live in Sweden for good. I was naïve to think that I could get a visa just like that because I'm a university student. We're not any better than others. We're not privileged. We have to struggle to get to where we want to be just like any other person."

"I agree," Tony said. "Now stop thinking and relax. Let's go get lunch."

"We can't go to Paris with you," said Ramzi. "And as I told you, our circumstances are really difficult; the situation with Sana and her parents are complicated."

"Even if I hadn't met Ramzi, my father would never let me go to Paris to study on my own. It's out of the question," said Sana in a sad tone.

"Yes, that's for sure," Ramzi said. "In any case, I have very little money right now. I'm really well paid as the body-guard of the Imam and have started saving, but it will take a while before I can approach Sana's parents."

"We understand," said Tony. "It probably was wishful thinking on our part that both of you could come with us."

"I promise that when the moment comes, I won't hesitate to join you in Paris with Sana. I'm hoping it will be in a year's time," Ramzi said and looked at Sana for support. She gave him one of her sweet, shy smiles. "I'm hundred percent with you my friends and I think you should leave. All four of you getting kidnapped and robbed the other day must truly be the last straw."

"On that subject, I have a favour to ask of you," said Waleed earnestly. "Now that you're in the inner circle of the Imam, is there any way you can procure a handgun for me? I'll feel a lot safer if I have something that will protect me. I'll pay whatever the cost."

"Don't start again, Waleed, please," said Carole.

"I'm serious," said Waleed, ignoring Carole's plea. "My parents are travelling in Europe and with the situation here they're not likely to return any time soon. I feel unsafe on a daily basis – I mean, being on my own. So, until I leave for Paris, I've got to feel secure. Otherwise, I'm going to go mad!"

"Alright, I think it's possible," said Ramzi after a long pause. "But I can't buy a handgun on my own. I don't want the Imam's people to think it's for me and I'm telling them a story. One of you has got to come with me. Let me make a phone call."

All five of them listened to Ramzi's coded phone conversation in astonishment. None of them had ever thought it was possible to buy a gun so easily.

"Okay. Here's the deal. A handgun in good working order is available with one of the suppliers in the southern suburbs. He's asking for 200 American dollars."

"That's fine. I've got the money for you at the ready," Waleed said. "When can we go?"

"Hold on. You can't come with me. Tony can't either. I know who I'm dealing with. It has to be a female – to soften the transaction. Sana can't be seen going there with me. It has to be one of you two," Ramzi said looking at Carole and Nora.

"I'll go with you," said Nora.

The next day, Ramzi picked Nora up in the afternoon. She'd never set foot in the southern suburbs of Beirut before. As Ramzi drove through the narrow streets, she couldn't imagine a place like that existed. There were very few new buildings here and there but almost every structure seemed akin to makeshift housing. The whole area, densely populated, was a large, sprawling shanty town. There were rows and rows of endless poor housing, so lacklustre and grey that she felt claustrophobic. Ramzi finally stopped the car in front of a tiny house that looked grey, too, because all one could see was the cement covering of the building – it had never been painted. They climbed up four steps and knocked on the door. A thin man in his early 40's opened the door and ushered them into a small sitting area furnished with armchairs covered in a garish coloured textile. Ramzi and Nora uneasily sat down.

"Our sister here wishes to buy it for her own protection," Ramzi said, looking at the man who sat opposite him. Ramzi slowly took the 200 dollars out of his pocket and placed it on the coffee table.

Nora looked down at her shoes, but hearing the commotion, looked up. She guessed they were the man's children. They stood at one side of the sitting room and stared at her and Ramzi. She counted five – the eldest must have been thirteen, the youngest probably five. The man's wife, a small woman with very fair skin and covered from head to toe except for her face and hands, brought three coffees on a tray and placed it on the coffee table. Without saying a word, she left promptly.

"Please enjoy your coffee," the man said. "Excuse me for a moment," and he left the room.

He returned a few minutes later with a handgun. It was such an awkward and surreal moment that Nora stopped listening to him. He was explaining how it worked. He showed Ramzi the cartridge and bullets, but all Nora wanted to do was to get out of there.

"You did great," Ramzi said on their way back to West Beirut. "It all went smoothly. Waleed will be very pleased."

"Why have you placed the gun next to you? Put it in the glove compartment," Nora said.

"You're not afraid of it, are you? Here, touch it if you want."

Accepting the challenge, Nora ran her fingers up and down the handgun but couldn't bring herself to actually hold it.

"What kind of gun is this?" She asked.

"Very common. It's Lebanese Internal Forces standard issue gun since the 1960's."

"Internal Forces? How did this man get hold of it?"

"Don't ask."

"So, what is it called, Ramzi?"

"Parabellum 9 mm."

CHAPTER 10
THE BASKETBALL TOURNAMENT

Carole first met Waleed when she was 15, and he 16, at a basketball tournament organized by a number of high schools in Beirut. The tournament venue that particular year was Waleed's high school. Carole was on her school's basketball team. Her teammates were, as usual, excited about tournaments. This was not only about the games but about the chance of meeting players from the opposite sex. Theirs was an all-girls' high school.

"How else are we going to meet boys?" Carole's classmate asked.

"Our lives are so boring – school, home, home, school… and not a single male in our lives," said another classmate.

"I'm betting on meeting my prince charming tomorrow," said another and sighed.

The following day, Carole's basketball team arrived at Waleed's high school for the start of the games. They were accompanied by a large group of schoolmates. The girls claimed they had come to cheer their school team. This was partly true, but they all had ulterior motives. Instead of sitting together in the audience, they had dispersed and Carole noticed them sitting next to boys from other schools in groups of three or four.

Waleed had come to just watch the games. He'd gone along with some of his classmates. He wasn't particularly interested in sports. Other than skiing with his parents, he had no interest in school sports. As soon as he sat down, he spotted a red-head walking past him and heading towards the centre of the playground. The spectators started cheering the players as they ran onto the court. The game began, and Waleed could not take his eyes off her. Who was she? He didn't think he'd ever seen her before. She was someone he would never forget if he'd encountered her previously. He watched all her moves. The way she ran, the way she passed the ball, and the way her pony-tail swung left to right. He couldn't understand his own sudden, obsessive behaviour. He had always been pursued by females and his attention span in response was always short. He had never been attracted to any girl this much before. He could not stop himself from looking at this wonderful creature.

At half-time, Carole finally noticed the person staring at her intensely. She did a double-take and was immediately attracted to the boy staring at her. All through the second half of the game she was conscious of his stare and hoped she wouldn't mess up her play. Carole's team won that day. They were to play again against another team the following day, and Carole somehow knew the boy would be there again. In the locker room, she told her mates about him and asked them to find out who he was.

"Out of your league," a classmate told her before the game started the following day.

"What? What do you mean?"

"He's one playboy who can't be trusted. His name's Waleed, and he's the rock star of his mixed gender high school. All the girls are in love with him. And they say he's a real snob. So, I would give him the brush if I were you."

Waleed was there again, seated at the same spot. Carole looked at him and he looked straight back at her. All through the game, he kept on staring at her without looking elsewhere. He did this quite discretely, Carole thought, or was it his long, curly hair that fell partly over his eyes that made it look like that. Carole's team lost the match that day. Her sad teammates left the basketball court one by one and headed towards the locker room. As she herself left and was nearing the locker room entrance, Waleed appeared at her side.

"I'm sorry you lost," he said, and grabbing her arm, placed a small piece of folded paper in the palm of her hand and gave her a half-smile.

He left without saying another word. She unfolded the paper. 'My name's Waleed. Call me'. She stared at the number and realized how happy she was – thrilled. She went into the locker room and said nothing to her teammates. She felt like calling him the minute she got home, but she stopped herself. It's too soon. She wasn't going to seem that easy. He had the guts to come up to her, but he didn't ask for her number. It was going to be up to her. She liked that. It was going to be her decision whether to call him or not.

She'd met a few other boys before, but every time it happened, she'd found something wrong with them. This guy's nose is too big. I don't like the way that one laughs. I can't stand the smell of his cheap cologne. She thought long and hard about Waleed. She couldn't fault him in any way. No wonder girls pursued him. He certainly had the looks and he was cool. She called him three days later.

"Hello, er...I'm Carole," she said shyly.

"I know who you are," he said.

He didn't have a car yet then. They met at a café in Hamra. She thought the date would last an hour at most but they were there for three hours, mainly talking about themselves and their interests. Carole did most of the talking. She'd ask a question and he would give her short answers but with no hesitation. She discovered they liked the same kind of music, movies, and food. At the end of that first date, it just felt so natural that they'd be together. And from that day onwards, they saw each other on a regular basis, usually at least once or twice on weekends.

It wasn't long before Carole knew she was in love with him. She was only fifteen then and like all young girls of her age was overly-jealous of the fact that he went to a mixed gender school and would see other girls during the week. Waleed, she knew early on, was not the type of guy who expressed sentiments easily. When he spoke, he used words sparingly. He was an introvert. She had to somehow find a way to enter into his world. And he was physically aloof. He had only held her hand once when they were watching a movie and gave her a kiss on her cheek on her birthday. A year into their relationship, she challenged him by saying he must be going out with other girls during the week. He was furious. That much she could sense. He was so enraged by what she'd said that he excused himself immediately and left, leaving her on her own at the café.

The next days were terribly painful for Carole. She thought she had lost him and didn't dare call him. It was Waleed who called her five days later.

"I missed you. Why didn't you call?" he said.

"I'm sorry about what I said," she mumbled. "Please forgive me."

"Forget the apology," he said. "*I want to see you tomorrow.*" He pronounced each of the words slowly, taking his time. He then added, "Can you make it at four at the café?"

When she got there the next day, Waleed was waiting for her outside the café.

"I want to take you to my place," he said.

"What?"

"Don't you want to see where I live? Don't worry. My parents are abroad. It's just me."

Carole was puzzled but she was not going to reject his invitation. When they got to his apartment, she felt awkward. This was the first time they'd been anywhere where they were completely on their own.

"Do you want me to make coffee?" Carole volunteered.

"No. Just sit down. I want to ask you something. Tell me frankly. Are you in love with me?"

"I...am" she said and knew that with her light skin, he would surely notice her blushing when her cheeks turned all red.

"I love you, Carole," he said looking into her eyes. "I love everything about you – your green eyes, your red hair, your freckles, everything."

For someone who had not expressed any of his feelings clearly since they first met, this was like a speech Carole longed he would be capable of giving. He now placed his hand on her neck and drew her close to him. He kissed her tenderly on the cheek. Carole focused on his dark eyes and then closing her eyes, kissed him on the lips. As if he'd been waiting a long while to express his powerful feelings for her, he now held her tightly and began to ardently kiss her. He then touched her breast and caressed and squeezed it gently. Carole suddenly felt out of breath.

"Let's not rush into this," she said, pushing him away.

"I'm sorry. You're right. We have all the time in the world. Eternity," he whispered and hugged her tightly.

"My love," she said softly in his ear.

When Carole first met Waleed, she didn't know that he didn't have close friends. True, he was admired by all who knew him for his musical talent and she was certain many girls had a crush on him and would have envied her. He had classmates he hung out with, but none of them were close. She soon realized that she was not only Waleed's lover, but his best friend, too. She met his parents and they were kind to her, but like Waleed, were aloof. She interpreted their behaviour as typical of upper middle-class or wealthy Lebanese. As she grew older and was freer to stay out late, she and Waleed became inseparable. But all Waleed wanted to do was be with her and play his guitar. He was antisocial and she made every effort to change that trait in him. It was Carole who insisted on him taking her to the DJ's events where they met Ramzi and Sana first and then Nora, Tony, and Michel. When the group of friends was formed, she congratulated herself in having succeeded in making Waleed more sociable and caring towards others. She was elated that Waleed responded to her wish and felt comfortable with their new group of friends. Their love affair grew and took the shape of an adult relationship.

Carole lost her virginity on a summer's day, a couple of months before the civil war began. It was on her 18th birthday. They had just returned to Waleed's apartment from a day at the beach with their group of friends. Waleed's parents were away in France. They had coffee together and then she asked Waleed to take her home.

"Stay a bit longer," he said, "It's still early. And it's your birthday. I've got something special to give you."

He dragged her into his bedroom.

"Close your eyes," he said and she obeyed.

He placed a silver chain with a cross pendant around her neck.

"I'm Druze, but you're Christian like my mother, not Jewish anymore." he said and kissed her.

"You're my first and last love," she said and hugged him.

"I want you, Carole," he whispered.

"Are you sure we're doing the right thing? I'm scared," she mumbled.

"Just relax. Let yourself go. I won't let you down."

He kissed her again. He hugged her and ran his fingers up and down her back. He then carried her and gently placed her on his bed.

He slowly started to undress her, all the while kissing her. She unbuttoned his shirt. She stopped. He continued undressing himself.

"What's the matter? I know we can't get hold of the pill in this country – not like in Europe, but don't worry, trust me, I'll be careful. In any case, if you fall pregnant, it will be our love child. I will love it like I love you. I will take the responsibility. Do you believe me?"

"Yes," she said firmly.

"Relax, my love," he said and began kissing her neck and then her breasts.

It all seemed so natural to her. She didn't have the inhibition she'd imagined she would have. Over the course of the previous two years, they had experienced physical intimacy but had stopped short of having full sexual intercourse. She had thought about the probability of this happening, and in her mind, she didn't think she had the confidence to go all the way with him. She now lost herself in his embrace. The short sharp pain she felt she quickly forgot as she placed her hands on his soft, olive-skinned broad shoulders that covered her like a protective shell.

When he moved away, she sat up and checked the bed sheet. There was a blood stain on it. Waleed saw it, too.

"Get up," he said and gathering the bed sheet, tossed it to one corner of the bedroom.

"I've soiled your bed sheet," she said, not knowing what else to say.

"I've soiled it too, so forget it. It's not important. Why are you crying? Did I hurt you?"

"No," she said, "I'm crying because...I'm happy."

"Come here," he whispered and pulled her towards him and held her tightly against his chest. "You're mine, Carole, forever."

CHAPTER 11
WALEED

Waleed was an only child and grew up a lonely kid. His father was from a prominent Druze family in Lebanon. A brilliant student, he had pursued postgraduate studies at Cambridge University before returning to Lebanon and establishing one of the top businesses in the country. Waleed's mother was from a middle-class Maronite Christian family. She had just completed a university degree when she took up a temporary position as Waleed's father's personal assistant. She was 12 years younger than her boss, but a mutual attraction led to a whirlwind romance and resulted in marriage. Marriage of two lovers from different religious communities was generally frowned upon in Lebanon except within the upper echelons of society where anything was permitted because of the power of wealth.

Waleed was born two years after his parents' marriage. He was never curious to ask them why they didn't have other children. He never felt close to them, especially emotionally. He did sometimes wish he had a brother. He was certain that his parents doted on him when he was an infant, judging by the number of pictures they took of him. But he didn't have any memories of his early childhood. He couldn't remember ever having met his grandparents, aunts, uncles, or cousins. His earliest memories were from his primary school days. He was mocked for being different from the rest of his classmates. The children were cruel and made fun of his mother for being Christian. They were the opposite of the chic ladies who visited his mother and never brought up the subject of religion. He never befriended his primary school classmates and kept himself to himself at school. The only time he interacted with other children was during holidays when his mother's chic lady friends would bring their children along to play with him or when he attended one of their birthday parties.

Waleed's parents provided him with everything he wanted. He had private tutors to help with homework. They bought him his first guitar at the age of 11 and took him on ski trips once or twice a year to the Alps in France or Switzerland. But they never spent real time with him. They talked to him about daily matters, school, private lessons, holiday plans, but never about anything personal. His father was constantly away on business. His mother never cooked a meal for him as they had a cook. All she cared about was her wardrobe, her make-up, and the visits to the hair salon. She cared more about her long, red-painted nails than she cared about him. She rarely displayed any affection towards him. And when she did, and this happened only occasionally, it was when it was his birthday or when she had to get him the fake ID. Waleed cocooned himself and made every effort to build his own world even though things improved with other students once he was sent to his prestigious high school. His salvation during puberty came in the guise of music and his guitar.

When he was 14, it suddenly dawned on him why his parents were the way they were. They had lost the love they had for each other and couldn't give him any. After all, he was the fruit of their dead love. And they were concerned about how people viewed them in their social circles and hypocritically displayed the appearance of a loving couple and family to the outside world.

"So, what do you do when you're travelling with Father," he dared ask his mother once.

"Oh, you know how he is. He's always busy with meetings and work. I just enjoy myself. I play bridge with my overseas acquaintances and shop," she replied.

When he was a little older, he suspected they probably had secret affairs, too, since they both virtually led separate lives. His mother was still young, attractive, and looked after herself; she gave herself the air of being born an upper-class lady. His father had the money to attract anyone eager to benefit from a relationship with him. His suspicions were based on the fact that their set of friends changed frequently. They never had long-term friendships. He remembered a dinner party his parents organized one New Year's Eve. That night his father gave over-the-top attention to a very tall, beautiful lady Waleed had never met before. She was an older woman, but he later found out she was single. She happened to be a famous journalist from a modest background who was known for being fiercely independent and anti-marriage. His mother didn't take one bit of notice of it, perhaps purposely, as she herself was constantly complemented by a man whose wife was not with him. The man had apologized for his wife's absence saying she had to attend another party at his in-laws. The man made sure he sat next to his mother at the table and smiled at her stupidly. Waleed disliked him the moment he met him. From that day onwards, whenever his parents organized dinner parties, he'd make sure he wasn't there.

Carole was the best thing that had happened to Waleed. Save for his music, his life was dull and empty before he met her. He did alright at school and was flattered that the girls at his high school pursued him, but he wasn't really interested in any of them. Carole was different. The moment he set eyes on her, he knew, instinctively, she was the one for him. He just didn't know the reason why. All he knew was that she was the breath of fresh air he was waiting for all his life. It was because of her that he had come out of his lonely cocoon and made friends. He saw her in his future, too. Un-cool as it may have appeared to him before he met her, he now dreamed of forming a family with her and having children. He was determined not to make his life similar to his parents'.

On the day of the kidnapping, Nora sensed something was wrong with Carole. She first thought it was the distress of getting kidnapped that made Carole look so depressed. Over the next few days, she asked her several times if everything was alright between her and Waleed or if she had any problems with her parents. Carole said all was fine but Nora wasn't convinced. Later, when they were alone one evening, Nora thought of asking her one last time.

"Carole, you're not your normal self. I know there's something bothering you."

"I've been meaning to tell this for days now but I didn't have the courage. What I'm going to say might shock you, Nora," said Carole, shutting the door of her bedroom after they returned from a long day out with Waleed and Tony. She looked terribly worried.

"Hey, come on. Tell me. You know nothing shocks me," Nora said.

"I think I'm pregnant," said Carole and burst into tears.

"What? I thought you said you took precautions."

"We did. I don't know how it happened but I've missed a period."

"Have you told Waleed?"

"No. And I don't plan to. That's why I'm telling this to you. I can't tell this to anyone else but you. I can't tell him, Nora. If I'm pregnant, I've got to get rid of it."

"But why won't you tell him? And if you're pregnant, why would you not want to keep the baby?"

"You don't know Waleed well enough," Carole said. "He would never allow me to have an abortion. I'm not ready to have a child right now. I'm only 18 for God's sake! I want us all to go to Paris and go to university. I can't have a child, Nora. And what am I supposed to tell my parents? Please, Nora, you've got to help me," said Carole, tears rolling down her cheeks.

"I don't know what to do, either," Nora said stunned.

"You've got to help me, Nora. I've got no one else to turn to."

"Alright. Please don't cry anymore. Let me think for a minute," Nora said and held Carole's hand to show her that she was on her side. And then she added, "I think I know the person who can help us."

That person was Layla, a mature university student who had taken several courses with them during the past academic year. She was in her late 30's and a divorcée with two teenage children. She was from a well-known and extremely well-to-do family in Beirut. And although she'd been living with her parents after her divorce, outside the house she lived a life with no holds barred. She attended all the hip parties and concerts in Beirut and was active in every sense. She had a regular boyfriend, quite a few years younger than her. She'd arrive to class on his Harley Davidson and both wore expensive leather outfits and helmets. She usually sat next to Nora and Carole during lectures and they had become friends. Once when they were talking about relationships, Layla had told them she had a perfect relationship with her boyfriend and great sex. If she weren't residing in Beirut, and because of her parents, she'd said, she'd be living with him without the constraints of marriage. In fact, Nora had called her the day after she'd arrived in West Beirut to get information about studying in Paris. Layla had siblings living in Paris and two cousins at university there.

Nora drummed up the courage to call her again. She explained the situation to Layla but didn't tell her the friend was Carole. Layla asked if they could meet the following day. Abortion was illegal in the country. Layla said she would recommend a gynaecologist who performed abortions but she didn't want to give his name on the phone. Nora went to meet Layla at a café the next day. Layla didn't ask her who the friend was but wondered whether the information was for Nora herself.

"Are you kidding? I'm still a virgin," Nora said.

"Okay. Sorry. Here's the doctor's name and address. He's the best. But it's going to cost you," Layla said and slipped a piece of paper into her hand before leaving.

Carole and Nora took an appointment and saw the gynaecologist two days later. They were surprised at his non-judgmental attitude. He didn't bat an eyelid – he'd seen it all before.

"You're seven weeks pregnant," he said to Carole. "I'm guessing you don't want to keep it."

"No, I don't."

"I can perform the abortion tomorrow morning. But you must be here before the clinic's regular opening time – 8 am sharp," he said in a business-like tone and then added, "This must remain confidential – you understand."

Both Carole and Nora responded with a nervous but firm 'Yes'.

"Are you sure you want to go through with this?" Nora inquired after they left the doctor's clinic.

"Nora, please. Don't do this to me. I'm 100% sure. Anyway, it's only seven weeks."

"He's charging an awful lot of money. How are we going to pay for it?"

"I've got the money," Carole said. "I've got some savings in the bank and I haven't touched that money in years."

"Listen, I can't go through this on my own. I think we need to tell Tony. He'll provide us the support we need."

"No! Please, let's just keep this between the two of us," Carole said.

"I can't be there for you without him. We need him. Carole, I promise he won't tell Waleed before it's done."

"Alright, I guess we do need his help – just in case," Carole conceded.

"Good. I have to call my parents and tell them I need to stay in West Beirut for another week. I need to look after you after it's done."

Nora called her parents as soon as they got back to Carole's apartment and told them she was waiting for information regarding Paris and needed to stay an extra week in West Beirut. She then called Tony at Waleed's and asked him to urgently come and see her at Carole's. She asked him not to tell Waleed. She said he should make up an excuse to leave. She told him she needed to see him alone.

"I can't believe you two have planned this. Don't you know abortion is illegal in this country? And risky, too!" said Tony angrily when they told him.

"The doctor's the best, we're told," Nora said.

"Tony, please, I need your help," Carole said and began to cry.

"Why are you keeping this a secret from Waleed? I don't understand. He'll never forgive us and God will never forgive you!"

"I don't want a child now, Tony. You can understand that much, can't you? If I tell Waleed, he'll stop me from having an abortion. I know it. He's got this romantic idea of us having many children. I mean, I don't mind having children later on in life but not now – not when we're planning on continuing our studies abroad. And think of my parents! It's my body and it's my decision!"

"You're jeopardizing your relationship with Waleed. Keeping something like this from him is not right," Tony tried to reason with Carole.

"That's what I told her, too. I know you will tell him once it's done, but putting him in front of a *fait accompli* could break your relationship beyond repair. And what makes you think he'll forgive you?" Nora said.

"I know Waleed better than you do. He'll forgive me no matter what! I'm sure. Please support me this once. I'm begging you."

"We won't let you down," Nora said and looked at Tony. Tony understood what she meant. Carole was in terrible distress. They had to assist her. They could not let her go through an abortion on her own.

"What time do you want me to pick you up tomorrow morning?" Tony inquired.

"At seven. We don't want to be late for the appointment," Nora said.

"Alright," he said. "But I'm not coming in with you. I'll wait for you outside the clinic even if it takes hours," Tony said and left promptly.

Waleed was rolling his 'hasheesh cig' as he had the habit of calling it when Tony returned to the apartment.

"So where have you been?"

"I just had coffee with Nora and Carole at the café around the corner from Carole's. Didn't want to disturb your siesta – you look pretty tired," Tony said.

"Yeah – I don't know why. I don't have much energy these days. Are we seeing Carole and Nora tomorrow?"

"That's what I was going to tell you. I think they have some kind of all girls' get-together – brunch or something. We'll call them in the evening," Tony said and felt embarrassed.

"Right. How about sharing my 'hasheesh cig'?"

"No, thanks. I wouldn't mind a glass of scotch though."

"Help yourself. Plenty at the bar – my parents keep buying those bottles. Someone has to drink them," said Waleed nonchalantly.

"Thanks. Oh, by the way, I need to see someone on behalf of my father tomorrow morning. I'll be leaving very early. Should be back by early afternoon."

"Okay. Let me get my guitar."

After pouring his scotch, Tony settled on the armchair opposite the sofa where Waleed was now sitting, holding his guitar. He began playing a sad, sentimental melody.

"That tune reminds me of Nora," Tony mused. "I think I love her. I haven't had the courage to make a confession all this time. I will have to tell her soon."

Waleed stopped and looked up, his curly hair falling on his eyes.

"Man, you're in love, for sure. My gut feeling is she loves you too – probably more than you love her. So don't delay it," Waleed said with a rare smile.

"How about you and Carole?"

"You know me – not much of a talker. I seldom tell anyone about my feelings, but I can tell you this. Carole is my oxygen. To me, life is meaningless without her. Without her I would be a fully-fledged depressive."

"You don't mean that. You're as normal as anyone else."

"I'm not. My friend, she is my saviour."

Waleed returned to playing his guitar. Tony nursed his drink, unable to say anything more. He had promised Nora and Carole not to tell Waleed. What else could he have done? He didn't know what the next day was going to be like. But this was akin to betraying a friend. He hated the feeling.

CHAPTER 12

FORGIVE AND FORGET

Tony waited for three hours outside the clinic, pacing up and down the pavement, before Nora and Carole reappeared. Both girls had gone in just before 8 am, looking like two frightened ducklings. When earlier on he had turned up at Carole's, he had witnessed Carole's tears. She was scared to go ahead with the abortion and Nora was cajoling her and using encouraging words, but she herself seemed extremely nervous. She kept cracking her knuckles – a sure sign she was terribly anxious. Tony knew Nora all too well not to recognize it. He had tried to comfort them as best he could on their way to the clinic, but the three-hour wait, and not knowing what was happening inside, had nearly killed him with worry. He now took comfort in seeing that both girls smiled at him, although Nora was holding Carole's arm tightly to provide her with the support she needed as she shuffled along.

"How did it go?" he asked, looking concerned.

"All went well," said Nora. "Let's get a cab."

"I'll do my part with Carole and her parents. We're going to say she's got a gut infection. I can administer the medication the gynaecologist gave her and make sure she's okay. But you've got to do your part. You're in charge of telling Waleed," Nora said when they were in the cab.

"Why me? Why not Carole herself?" Tony said indignantly.

"Are you joking? She's in a very fragile state right now. She has to rest for a few days at home. How are we going to explain that to Waleed? You have to tell him, Tony, please," Nora said.

"Don't do this to me, Nora," he said, but Nora's beautiful eyes, looking straight into his, had already disarmed him.

"Alright, alright, I'll do what you want, but I'm not responsible if he reacts negatively. Don't blame me if it happens."

"No one's going to blame you for anything, Tony. I'm grateful for what you did today," Nora said and gave him one of her sweet smiles.

He would have done anything for that smile. His fondness of Nora grew day by day and he felt he was lucky to have her as a friend. He had to work on making her his lover for good. When he reached Waleed's apartment, he felt more confident to tell him about Carole's abortion. He found Waleed in the kitchen preparing his breakfast. He had just woken up late, as usual.

"Hey! You're back! How was your morning?" he asked.

"Alright," Tony said and headed towards the sitting room.

"Are we seeing the girls this afternoon or evening? I miss Carole so much these days, I sometimes can't believe it," he said with a serious tone and joined Tony in the living room carrying his plate of apricot jam and toast.

"I don't think we can see them today either."

"Why?"

Tony stood silent for a while, lowering his head.

"What's the problem? Is there something wrong? Is there something you're not telling me?"

"I was with Nora and Carole this morning."

"Why didn't you tell me? I would've come along."

"Carole had an abortion this morning."

Waleed froze. What was going on in his head now? What was he thinking? Tony thought Waleed's eyes had turned blood red. They were partly hidden behind his curly locks and Tony couldn't be sure. Even if he had spoken softly, had he gone too far by telling Waleed so directly? He felt awkward but decided to apologise to break the silence.

"I'm sorry, Waleed. Carole and Nora asked me yesterday not to tell you before it was done."

"That girl is going to fucking kill me one of these days," Waleed said angrily after a very long silence.

"She said you wouldn't let her go through with it if she told you beforehand."

"She's right. I wouldn't have. And thanks for not telling me," Waleed said sarcastically. His face took on the expression that he was in awful pain – one that had spread all through his body.

"Don't be like that. Please understand her. Don't be so selfish."

"Enough said!" Waleed yelled. He abruptly left the living room for his bedroom and slammed the door shut.

Tony sat in the living room for a good half hour and didn't know what to do next. Should he try to talk to Waleed again? He wasn't certain it was a good idea. The news of the abortion had certainly shaken him badly. It was best to let Waleed calm down before attempting another conversation with him. He left the apartment and went for a walk around Hamra, dazed, trying not to think about anything in particular. His footsteps eventually led him to Carole's apartment block.

"Did you tell Waleed?" was the first thing Nora asked him when he entered Carole's bedroom. Carole was sitting in bed and smiled at him as if nothing had happened.

"I'm alright. In fact, I feel I'm back to normal. I feel like going out," Carol said cheerfully.

"She's doing remarkably well," added Nora. "She'll be out and about in a couple of days."

"Did you tell Waleed?" This time it was Carole who asked him the question.

"I did. But...he was very angry. I think you need to talk to him as soon as possible."

"I'll go and talk to him right now," she said.

"You need to rest for another day at least," protested Nora. "Let's go see him tomorrow. Give him at least a day to calm down. He's too angry to see you now," she added.

Tony bought some food and went back to Waleed's apartment. Waleed's breakfast plate was still on the coffee table in the living room. He cleared it and was sure Waleed had not come out of his bedroom while he was gone. He knocked on his bedroom door and asked him to join him for dinner. There was no sound. He knocked again – this time louder.

"Leave me alone, will you?" came the reply.

"For your information, Carole is doing fine. She's coming to see you tomorrow," he shouted.

Waleed mumbled a reply, but Tony couldn't make out what he said. He went and sat at the dining table. He had a couple of mouthfuls and gave up on eating. He sipped the scotch he had poured himself and hoped the next day was going to be a better day.

Carole and Nora arrived at Waleed's apartment in the early afternoon the next day. Tony had barely said hello to them when Waleed opened his bedroom door and walked straight up to Carole, who was still standing in the living room. He lunged over and gave Carole a slap on the face. She was so taken aback that her mouth and green eyes opened as wide as they possibly could.

"What the hell are you doing?" yelled Nora. Waleed turned his gaze towards her.

"Hey! Calm down!" Tony said.

"What do you think you're doing to a girl who's just had an abortion and is in a fragile state? Shame on you! Come to your senses, Waleed. Carole can't have a child now – get that into your dense head!"

"Nora, please," said Tony to make her stop.

Without uttering a word, Waleed tenderly touched Carole's hair that had fallen over her face. Carole, who had taken on the expression of a guilty little girl, said "I'm sorry" with downcast eyes. Waleed immediately grabbed her by the wrist and whisked her to his bedroom, shutting the door.

"I'm scared. Do you think he might hurt her?" asked Nora.

"No. Let's give them the chance to make up," Tony said and dragged Nora to the balcony.

It was a couple of hours later that Carole re-appeared. She seemed fine, except for her swollen eyelids. She had cried a good deal.

"You're not hurting, are you?" said Nora.

"No, no, I'm alright. I haven't felt better," she replied.

"Everything okay with Waleed?" asked Tony.

"Yes," she said and then added, "I'm really feeling much better. You guys can go back to East Beirut. No need to worry about me."

Nora looked at Tony. It did seem that Waleed and Carole had made up.

"How about us going back not tomorrow but the following day?" Nora asked Tony.

"Yes, that's okay as long as Waleed and Carole are alright," Tony said.

"Where's Waleed? Is he not coming out of his room?"

"It's been...exhausting...don't mind him. Let's go," Carole said firmly.

"Hey, are you sure you won't have any more trouble with Waleed?" asked Nora on their way to Carole's.

"Nora, don't worry. All's back to how it was between us."

"Thank God!"

Waleed didn't come out of his bedroom that night. But Tony didn't mind. Things must have worked out between Waleed and Carole. Otherwise, he wouldn't be playing his guitar, Tony thought.

The next morning, Tony was surprised to see Waleed up and about at 10 am. He didn't say much – just 'good morning' and a few other casual sentences. Tony felt relieved and asked if they could go for a ride in Waleed's car.

"Let's," Waleed said and then casually added, "The house is going to feel empty when you've gone back to East Beirut. I got used to you being around."

⋙⊹⊱

Earlier in Waleed's bedroom
Waleed forced Carole to sit on his bed even when she protested that she'd rather stay standing up. A very long silence followed. Carole was afraid to say anything lest she'd be misunderstood or say something that could upset him even more. She didn't even dare look at his face. She waited for Waleed to start the conversation. She knew she had to wait. Words didn't come to him easily. Waleed, who remained standing, finally came over and sat next to her. They both stared at the Persian carpet that lay on one side of his bed.

"You betrayed me," he said in a tone that revealed his disappointment in her. "I don't know if I should forgive you for doing it behind my back. And it's not something that can be taken lightly. It's something really serious." And raising his voice, he said, "Why did you do it?"

"Waleed, please understand my situation. I was seven weeks gone – how am I to explain that to my parents? And how am I supposed to look forward to studying abroad when I'm pregnant? I knew you would have stopped me from getting rid of it."

"Getting rid of it? I don't care about that religious nonsense, but you've killed the fruit of our love. Are you happy now?"

"I *am* really sorry, Waleed. I swear I would not have done it if we weren't in the current circumstances. There's a war going on. I want to be with you in Paris. I want to enjoy us as a couple. I want to go to university with you. I don't think having a baby at this stage is wise. We can have as many babies as you want once we've finished our studies," she said, holding back her tears. This was not the time to show weakness.

"What makes you think we will be together in the future after what you've done?" he said. That was a typical Waleed statement – the aloof, uncaring character that people identified him as. Was this the real Waleed? Carole broke into a sweat. Was all the love he had shown her thus far a farce? Could this be the end of their fairy tale love story? She felt dizzy and her face turned all white.

"Are you alright? You look very pale. Shall I get you some water?" Waleed said softly. His anger seemed to have dissipated.

"I just feel a bit dizzy. I'm fine. I don't need anything."

Waleed suddenly held her hand and for the first time looked at her face.

"I'm sorry I slapped you. Forgive me – I couldn't control my anger. I'm sorry I've seemed unconcerned about you and didn't ask you how you were."

"I'm really okay. Don't worry about me. Nora's been looking after me very well."

"I'm glad," he said. He played with his curly hair with his free hand as if to shape it and then sighed. "I'm resentful that I was excluded from all this, but I understand your reason for doing so. I wrecked my brain all of last night until the small hours of the morning. It still hurts though.

But tell me exactly how, where, and when it was done and by whom."

When Carole had finished recounting all the details of having the abortion, she said, "I'm sorry again." She remembered what he told her earlier on and drumming up the courage she added, "But if you don't trust me anymore, let's end it here."

There was a long silence again and Waleed let go of her hand. Was this really the end? Carole felt weak and defeated. But what Waleed did next, she could never have imagined. He hugged her so tightly that she was almost out of breath. Still hugging her, he began to cry. It was not just crying – it was as if he were wailing. She could never have imagined him crying like a baby. The aloof snob that he portrayed to the outside world was capable of being a sensitive, caring being and showing intense emotions. She could no longer hold back her tears and began crying too.

"How could you ever imagine life without me?" he finally said, releasing her and looking deep into her eyes. His tears kept rolling down his cheeks. It reminded Carole of the teenager with the angelic gaze who stared at her at the basketball tournament three years ago.

"I thought you would never forgive me and that you would end our relationship," she said, sobbing.

"No matter what happens, I will love you till the end of time. Never forget that. And I promise I will look after you," he said wiping his tears and hers. "Promise me that you will trust me always."

"I promise," she said and felt guilty for doubting him. She promised herself then that she would never again doubt him or fear him no matter what the future had in store for them.

"This is something we've never experienced before. I don't want a repeat of this ever again. I'm begging you to come to me with your problems and fears from now on. And I will never oppose your decisions."

He then drew her close to him and kissed her tenderly on the lips, squeezing her shoulder gently with one hand and holding the back of her head with the other. He next asked her to lie down on the bed.

"You must be tired. Rest a bit."

Carole obeyed him. Waleed lay next to her and ran his fingers through her hair.

"Are you in pain at all?"

"No. I didn't feel anything even then. I guess the doctor gave me sedatives. I just feel a bit fragile, that's all."

Waleed reached for her belly area and gently caressed her.

"I'm sorry for what you went through," he said and his eyes welled up again.

Carole held her hand out and pulled him towards her. She kissed his tears and then his lips.

"Let's not cry anymore," she said.

Waleed hugged her tightly and she felt safe in his arms again.

CHAPTER 13

THE YOUNG MAN AT THE PARIS FLEA MARKET

Spring 1978

When Nora first set eyes on the young man standing in front of his little stand at the Paris flea market in the Porte de Clignancourt, she could never have imagined he would be the father of her daughter. It was very cold that year in Paris, and the cool weather had stretched way into spring. She was wearing her fur-trimmed heavy coat still, and unlike her usual comportment, had put on a lot of makeup and wore a pair of high-heeled boots. It was the influence of her then roommate at the Armenian House of the Cité Universitaire, the university student dormitory campus, at the edge of Paris, located near the Porte d'Orléans; the gated grounds, where many countries had built their own prestigious buildings to house students, were full of tall trees, manicured lawns, and gardens with flower beds. It was the nicest place for a student to live in Paris. Nora felt lucky to have secured a place there and had obtained a grant from an Armenian benevolent association to pay the rent.

And she felt even more fortunate to finally have an Armenian student from Beirut to share the room with. Her previous roommate was a strange Vietnamese student who was, unfortunately, mentally unstable. Nora hadn't met anyone like her before and didn't know how to deal with her. The director of the Armenian House had assured Nora that it was a temporary arrangement and that the Vietnamese student would soon be leaving the house for psychiatric treatment in a reputable institution. Nora never had a proper conversation with the Vietnamese student and she wasn't even sure what her real name was. Everyone knew her as Titi. Titi's grumpiness, nervous ticks, and murmuring to herself drove Nora crazy. But coming from a war-torn country herself, Nora understood that Titi must have gone through serious trauma back in Vietnam. The only problem was that Titi had the habit of waking up in the middle of the night and hovering around Nora's bed. She woke Nora up on several occasions. When Nora opened her eyes, she could make out Titi's face in the dark. It was only inches away from hers. She shooed Titi away every time, but she was scared to death, thinking that Titi may strangle her in her sleep one of these days.

The Vietnamese Titi was replaced by the Armenian Sonia. Sonia was the complete opposite of her previous roommate. Vivacious, always joking, experimenting with clothing and makeup, Sonia was full of life and wanted to visit places of interest in Paris in the weekend. Nora welcomed Sonia's presence. She made her happy. She had felt so lonely in the past month that she even thought of not finishing her academic year and going back to Beirut. Tony had been completely ignoring her. She couldn't believe this was happening to her and their relationship. True, they were busy with their studies at different universities in Paris with different schedules, and Nora was babysitting almost every afternoon and evening including Saturdays sometimes to supplement her student income. Tony had stopped passing by at night to say hello like he often used to. One Saturday, she and Sonia had gone to one of the university restaurants on the grounds of the Cité for lunch. She bumped into Tony and Carole as she and Sonia were leaving the restaurant. She said 'Hi' to them but there was an awkward pause and Tony said he'd come and visit her soon before the two of them quickly moved on. She felt that Carole wanted to stop and talk to her but that Tony somehow prevented her from doing so. Why was Tony acting so coldly towards her? Nora tried to reason that Tony must have his valid reasons for not turning up at her place and naively believed that everything between them would be back to the way they were. She'd soon discover that that could never be.

After Tony and Carole had left for Canada, Nora had felt constantly anxious and depressed. It was Sonia who had come to her rescue. Her happy and optimistic nature was contagious. She'd make plans to do things together whenever Nora had free days. On that fateful Sunday, both Nora and Sonia walked into their favourite café/restaurant, all decked out. It was the Lido's café on the Champs Elysées which was still affordable then even for students – although only as a splurge. They frequented it almost every other

Sunday for lunch and each had a *Salade Niçoise* followed by *La Bombe,* a French dessert that had a mountain of vanilla ice cream, covered in chocolate sauce, placed in the centre of a plate. Sonia suggested they go to the Paris flea market afterwards. She was all excited about looking for a pair of second-hand retro sunglasses.

Nora approached Xavier's stand, attracted by the hand-made costume jewellery displayed on the small stand. She liked a pair of earrings and looked up to ask the price. She had not set eyes on such a handsome young man before. Xavier stood tall behind his stand. He sported the bohemian-look that was so in vogue at the time. He was lean with long blond hair and almost turquoise eyes that would have turned the head of any girl. He looked at her intently whilst he was quoting the price and explaining how he had made the earrings. After Nora bought the pair of earrings, he gave her his visiting card and, to Nora's surprise, asked for her phone number. She told him that she was a student and that there was only one shared phone on the floor of her dorm at the Cité Universitaire. He said he knew right away she was a university student and that it didn't matter where the phone was as long as he had the number to contact her. He said he didn't mind waiting on the line until she could get to the phone.

The following night, someone knocked on Nora's door and said there was a phone call for her. Nora literally ran to answer the phone which was anchored to the wall at the end of her floor corridor. The night before, Sonia had told her that she was lucky for Xavier's sort of guy to be interested in her. She'd told Sonia she didn't want to flatter herself and that there was no way the guy would call her.

"Hi! It's Xavier from yesterday." He spoke to her in English.

"Hi! But why are you speaking to me in English and not French?" Nora inquired.

"You were talking to your friend in English yesterday and I just want you to know I speak English, too. I'm a university student – third year. Do you want to go to an Irish pub with me on Saturday night? There are many people who speak English there."

Nora was overwhelmed by the emotion that someone was that interested in her and especially someone like Xavier. She had never been one of those Lebanese girls whose sole aim in life, instilled in them by their parents, was to look as attractive as possible to find a suitor. Nora did not have the awareness that she was a very attractive young woman. In fact, decades later Tony would reveal to her that many guys were interested in her in Lebanon but couldn't approach her because they were apprehensive that she would reject them. To many young men in Beirut, she was as inaccessible as she thought Xavier was to her.

Like a true gentleman, Xavier picked her up from the Cité and took her to the Irish pub on Saturday. They enjoyed each other's company so much that they stayed at the pub until closing time and missed the last metro. He called a university friend of his who lived nearby and asked her if they could crash out at her studio. And although Nora felt awkward to be sleeping at a stranger's place, Xavier tried to make her feel as comfortable as possible. They shared a mattress on the floor. They slept next to each other but Xavier didn't even attempt to kiss her. All he said was that he enjoyed being with her and then placed his hand tenderly on her cheek.

Nora saw Xavier the following weekend. He was an amateur photographer and took a lot of photos. 'Can I take a photo of you some time?' he said in the metro as they were returning from their date. 'I would specially like to photograph your beautiful, large, dark eyes', he added. Nora said yes, but she was embarrassed. She never liked being photographed. A couple of days later, it was Nora who called him this time. She said the Armenian House was organizing a photography exhibition and asked Xavier if he would be interested in exhibiting some of his photographs. Xavier immediately said yes. The next day, Nora introduced him to the manager of the Armenian House who gave Xavier the go ahead to set up his display of photographs in the designated hall. There were displays of the works of other amateur photographers and the event, which ran over three days, proved successful with more than the expected number of visitors. Xavier was elated and gladly accepted to join Nora and other students from the Armenian House for a dinner and dance party that was taking place in-house on the final day of the exhibition.

There were copious amounts of Armenian food, lots of wine, and Armenian folk music at the party. Nora was happy to see that for Xavier all this was a novelty but that he was enjoying himself. He even joined Nora and others at one point when they began to dance the circular Kochari Armenian folk dance and attempted to mimic their dance moves. The party dragged on until the small hours of the morning. Most of the students were drunk by then and one by one left for their rooms. Xavier and Nora were the sober-est of the lot. Xavier remarked that he had missed the last metro again and asked if he could sleep in Nora's room. When they got to Nora's room, Sonia was already in bed and was snoring, having had too much to drink.

Xavier and Nora lay squeezed side by side in Nora's single bed. Xavier suddenly rolled Nora over and she now lay partly on top of him. He gave her a tender look and kissed her. 'You're so beautiful', he said and kissed her again. They kissed over and over again. He caressed her hair and back and kissed her once more. He then took her hand and placed it between his legs. The minute she felt that he had a massive hard on, Nora panicked. What was she doing? She was frightened because she felt gauche. She had very little experience with men apart from her experience with Tony. And then she realized that although she was very much attracted to Xavier, it was Tony that lived in her heart. She pulled her hand away and apologized. 'I can't do it…I'm still a virgin…My Middle Eastern background won't allow me to…maybe if we were in a steady relationship…' She said these sentences mechanically as if she were shooting bullets one after the other. Xavier smiled and kissed her on the forehead. He said that they had just recently met and that he understood, but his voice betrayed disappointment. 'Sleep', he said and she fell asleep on his chest.

The next morning when Nora got up, Sonia was already gone and had left her a note, saying that she was going shopping to buy a pair of shoes. Nora quickly set up a breakfast of cheese, jam, and baguette on the small table. Xavier was still asleep. When she brought the water that she'd boiled on her small electric stove from the ante room, Xavier was up and sitting on the chair next to the table. 'Come here', he said pulling her over and making her sit on his lap. He rocked her like a baby, all the while caressing her arms, her face, her hair. 'Your face is so pretty. I can't stop looking at you', he said. He gave her one final kiss and said he was ready to go. Nora insisted he should have breakfast. He said he wasn't hungry. He dressed and left quickly. A few minutes later, she looked out of her window and there he was – leaving the building. He looked up and noticing her, waved her goodbye.

Xavier didn't call her after that day. And Nora stopped going to the Paris flea market. She couldn't bring herself to go there. She believed he was looking for a woman with sexual experience, not a naïve Middle Eastern girl like her. Of all the guys she'd met in Paris after Tony's departure, Xavier was still the one that she was attracted to the most. He kept on popping up in her head, but she had behaved in such an embarrassing way towards him that it was difficult to turn the clock back.

Nora was genuinely flattered that men were interested in her and the whole male experience was like a new discovery. In those student days in Paris, one could meet a new guy every day if one wanted to. There were the good ones like the German student with the cherubic face who gave her the sweetest kiss she'd experienced and the Dutch 'rocker' student who was the coolest guy she'd met. Sadly, they both had to go back to their hometowns. Then there were the bad ones like the Corsican who sang his native songs at the top of his voice after a couple of drinks and who tried to kiss her like a brute, but she managed to push him away and put an end to the relationship. And there was the older English professor who invited her to expensive restaurants in the hope of starting a relationship with her, but who failed abysmally.

She met Xavier again by pure chance, or so she thought, at the university restaurant at the Cité. Two years had elapsed since they last saw each other.

"Hi! It's been a long while!" It was Xavier walking towards her with his tray of food.

"Hi! I didn't know you frequented this university restaurant. And you must have graduated a long time ago," Nora said shyly surprised at seeing him there.

"Yea, I only eat here if I can procure university restaurant tickets from somebody. Meals are still the cheapest in Paris here. May I sit down?"

And that's how it all re-started. Xavier soon confessed to her that he had actually sought her out and knew which university restaurant she regularly ate at. He said he couldn't forget the Armenian girl with the pretty face. They began going out regularly for a month and then the relationship turned into romance and became serious. Xavier asked her to come and live with him in his studio flat. And Nora, for the first time since Tony left Paris, began burying him deep in her heart.

Xavier didn't believe in marriage. His bohemian appearance matched his outlook on life. Nora in reality didn't care for marriage either. She had already started shedding her Middle Eastern inhibitions and had internalized the European way of conducting relationships. But she knew that her parents would disapprove of 'cohabitation' – a word that the French liked to use. It was her last year at university and she wholeheartedly embarked on a new life with Xavier. He still hadn't found a regular job but did the flea market at the weekend and had a part-time job as a photographer's assistant. Nora didn't care what he did as long as they could get by. She was proud of him and thought she was fortunate to have the affection of such a handsome man.

And then she fell pregnant.

CHAPTER 14
AURORE ARSHALUYS

Nora and Xavier's romance faded away as quickly as it had started. Nora had an inkling of how things might turn out on the first day she moved in with Xavier. She intuitively knew he would not be loyal to her in the long run. He'd shown her tenderness and intimacy and given her the experience of carnal pleasures. She'd finally felt like a full-fledged adult. But the relationship would be temporary. In a way, she thought that that was all she deserved from the relationship anyway. She was aware that she would not be able to give him her full loyalty either. She still thought about Tony despite herself and wondered if he would have been happier had he married her instead of Carole.

She found out she was pregnant a week before graduation. When she told Xavier, he was happy enough but not overly enthusiastic about becoming a father. He was affectionate towards her as usual and accompanied her on her regular doctor's visits, but he started to become distant as her belly grew bigger every day. By her sixth month, he was already coming home very late at night or sometimes not coming home at all. When she complained, he begged her not to become like a nagging wife. His excuse was that he was trying to earn more money for the baby by doing party and wedding photography. Nora realized that in her condition, she couldn't depend on him. What if her pains occurred at night while he was away? She asked him if she could have her mother come over from Beirut to help her during the later months and after delivery. He agreed immediately. But he said he would have to move out of the studio and stay with a friend to give her mother the space she needed.

Nora's mother arrived when Nora was gone eight months. Her mother was happy to be there and be with her daughter but she frowned upon the relationship. 'You're going to give birth soon and you're not even married! Lord, have mercy!' she kept on repeating. No matter how much Nora tried to explain to her that cohabitation was a normal thing in France, her mother refused to accept the idea. The concept was too alien for her. And she didn't like Xavier. When Nora confronted her one day, she barked at her and said, 'He doesn't have a proper job. How is he going to look after you and the baby? And he's too *pretty* – he will have women running after him all the time. You mark my words!'

When Nora's labour pains began one evening, Xavier wasn't there to take her to the hospital. Nora struggled for 12 hours to give birth. She was obviously upset that Xavier wasn't beside her, so her mother tried to appease her, give her all the help she could and support her in her pain. She gave birth to a baby girl at dawn. The absent father turned up at noon. The first thing he said after Nora gave him the baby to hold was, 'What are we going to name her?'

"Arshaluys – dawn in Armenian. She was born at dawn!"

"That's a nice name. I like it," Xavier said then added, "But it'll have to be her second name since it is the custom in France to give a newborn two names. We need to give her a first French name."

"Aurore then – dawn in French."

Aurore Arshaluys became Nora's only *raison d'être*. She breathed Arshaluys, adored Aurore, dreamed of her and thought about her every single moment of the day. It no longer mattered to her if Xavier was around or not. She breast-fed her for a short while but couldn't continue for lack of sufficient milk. She slept very little the first three months but she was grateful to her mother who extended her stay by a couple of months to give her the breather she needed during the day. All this while Xavier was staying at the studio of a friend and after her mother left, he didn't move back in with her. He gave Nora the lame excuse that his sleep would be disturbed by the baby's cries and he couldn't function at work if he hadn't slept sufficiently.

When Aurore Arshaluys was six months old, things began to deteriorate even further between Xavier and Nora. She accused him of not giving her enough money to live on and Xavier said that was the best he could do. Thus, Nora began looking for a job and found one after her third attempt. She started as a translator/interpreter at a very large PR company. But who was to look after the baby? For the first time in a long while Xavier seemed to care about her situation. He said he would gladly babysit the baby while Nora went to work. He worked nights and weekends anyway he said. He didn't come home at night but did turn up every morning before Nora went to work. The arrangement suited them both – she had a babysitter father and he didn't have to worry about supporting his child. Nora's heart broke every day to leave the baby at home and go to work though. She missed Aurore Arshaluys terribly, but there was no other way. They had to survive on her regular income. And at least she knew her daughter was in the safe hands of her father.

This went on for a good two years until, one day, upon her return from work Xavier announced that he was leaving France.

"Where are you going?"

"To the island of Guadeloupe. Some friends and I are going to open a bar there."

"And who's going to look after your daughter?"

"Don't be difficult, Nora. You know I'm a free spirit. And I've done my bit. You can send her to a nursery and it won't be long before she goes to kindergarten."

Before Xavier's departure, Nora found out from a common friend that one of Xavier's friends involved in the project of the bar in Guadeloupe was in fact Xavier's current lover. It surprised Nora that the news didn't have an effect on her. She didn't even feel jealous. The behaviour was one she must have expected from Xavier. Ever since the birth of her daughter, they had stopped being a couple. And she was certain he'd been sleeping with other women from the day she announced she was pregnant.

Xavier left for Guadeloupe a few months later. He came over to France to see his daughter only once in the next ten years. And he never sent her any money. The burden of looking after their daughter was squarely on Nora's shoulders. She initially found a nanny, an older woman, and afterwards, a succession of babysitters who picked her daughter up from nursery school or kindergarten. It wasn't easy for Nora to juggle work and motherhood but she never complained. She was doing everything she possibly could for her daughter. She moved up the ladder in the PR company fairly quickly too and became a junior middle management employee in three years.

As time went by, Nora began to feel terribly lonely. The older Aurore Arshaluys got, the lonelier she felt. She started to feel sorry for herself, too. After putting her daughter to bed every night, she'd sit and think about everything that made her unhappy: The curse of being a descendant of genocide survivors, the sadness of leaving her birthplace because of war, the tough everyday life of single motherhood. She should have been happy. Aurore Arshaluys was growing up ever so quickly and she was a beautiful child – she had the exact facial traits of her father and the same body shape – the only difference between them was Aurore's darker hair. And Nora was doing extremely well at work. Why was she unsatisfied with her life? She realized she had got into a chronically depressive state and was in two minds whether she should see a shrink like so many French people did. A colleague, who'd become a close friend, and who knew her situation, advised Nora to go on a singles' holiday instead – just for a week. Maybe she'll meet someone new there, she said. The friend offered to look after her daughter whilst she was away. Nora, encouraged by her friend's offer to babysit

Aurore, eventually booked a week's holiday for the first time in her life.

That's how she met Bertrand. Just out of a traumatic divorce, he seemed subdued and gentle. Nora felt comfortable around him. Their relationship blossomed quietly and before long Bertrand asked her to move in with him. 'I've got a three-bedroom large apartment. My marriage didn't produce any children and I consider your daughter like my own. Why not live with me?' Nora accepted Bertrand's offer. Her daughter, who was nine years old at this time, initially liked Bertrand and Nora reasoned they would have a semblance of a family life if they lived together. This vision of hers did come true for a few years. They would go on family lunch trips outside Paris, take family type of holidays in the south of France, and spend joyous Christmases.

Things began to sour when Aurore Arshaluys went into puberty. She started to hate Bertrand. She found him overbearing and strict with her, meddling in everything she did and putting her down constantly. Nora was caught between the two of them, trying to pacify one side and then the other. One Sunday evening a fighting match broke out between the two over her daughter being late coming back home. She'd gone to a friend's house to study for an exam. When Bertrand chided Aurore, she answered back and then shouted, 'You're not my father. Stop telling me how to behave'. Bertrand then slapped her. Aurore ran to her room and locked the door behind her.

"We need to get married. I need to officially adopt her," Bertrand said after he'd calmed down.

"We'll talk about it," Nora said. "Let me try and pacify her first."

Nora stood in front of her daughter's bedroom and begged her to open the door. Her daughter eventually did. Nora sat on her daughter's bed and asked her to come and sit down next to her.

"Why are you so aggressive and combative towards Bertrand?"

"He's always giving me a hard time. I resent it. I hate him. He's not my father!"

"Would you have the same behaviour if he adopted you and became officially your father?"

"Mum, you're not going to marry him, are you? Mum, you don't love him!"

Nora was stunned. Her 14-year-old daughter saw the reality of things. She was sharp, sensitive, and observant. Nora had tried to ignore her feelings towards Bertrand for a long time. At the beginning of their relationship, she was flattered by the attention he gave her and he was very kind towards her daughter. But as years went by, and the routine of everyday life set in, she knew she had no more feelings left for him in her heart. He had just asked her to consider marrying him. She had to find a way of telling him she couldn't. For the sake of the five years of living together, the least she could have done is to tell him the truth and stop living a lie.

"Have you thought about what I said the other day," Bertrand asked her on the Friday night when her daughter had gone out to the cinema with her classmates.

"I have. I don't think I can," she said sheepishly.

"Why? What's the problem? We've been living together for five years and the marriage will seal our union. It's better for your daughter as well."

"I just can't."

"You're saying you don't love me anymore."

Nora couldn't tell him she'd never been in love with him. That would have really hurt and destroyed him.

"It's difficult to express myself," she said, dodging the issue. "I do care about you a great deal."

"Okay. Let's forget about marriage if it makes you uncomfortable. Let's stay as we are," he said with a tone that betrayed disappointment.

"I don't think we can go on like this either," she blurted out.

"Stop saying absurdities," he said, now clearly upset.

"Bertrand, I'm serious. I think we need to end our relationship. I'll move out as soon as I find an apartment to rent."

"Is this because I'm having conflicts with your daughter? You know it's her age – it's a passing thing. Everything will be alright soon."

"It's not that. It's unfair to you if I hang around for longer. If I can't be enthusiastic about marrying you, then it means my heart is not in the right place. Do you understand that? You need to find someone who wants to spend the rest of her life with you. Please let me go," she pleaded with him quietly.

Bertrand, angry, began a litany of accusations. He was throwing a tantrum, bringing up all sorts of disagreements between them from the past and blaming her for this and that. She didn't answer back – she was no longer listening. He finally got up from his armchair and walked towards the door. He left the apartment, slamming the door behind him. All Nora heard him say was 'You're cursed!'

That night Nora slept with her daughter. She heard Bertrand come in very late. She heard him stagger. He must have been drunk. She heard a thump. She got up to check on him. He was sound asleep in bed, face down. The next day, she packed a bag each for her and her daughter and they stayed in a hotel. She left a note for Bertrand, telling him she'd be picking up her stuff in the next few days.

Nora found an apartment not far from her daughter's school. Her daughter could walk to school – she was delighted. It wasn't going to be easy packing her things at Bertrand's place while he was there, so she took a few days off from work and did her packing during the day when Bertrand was at work. He must have noticed her things disappearing when he came home at night. He must have gathered she had meant what she'd said and she was not going to change her mind. He left her a note on the kitchen table telling her to please tell him goodbye in a civilized manner. Although she'd packed everything she needed to the next day, she wrote him a reply and said she'd come again specially to bid him farewell on the following Sunday afternoon.

"I've come to say goodbye. I won't be staying long, Bertrand," she said when he opened the door.

"Come in, don't just stand there."

She took a few steps in and stopped.

"I really want to tell you I'm sorry if I hurt you. I truly am. I want to thank you, too, for caring about me and my daughter. I hope with all my heart that you will find the love you deserve. You're a good man."

Bertrand pulled her over and hugged her.

"I can't force you to stay," he said, still hugging her. "I hope you find happiness in your life."

He now let her go. 'Call me if you need anything, anything at all', he said, making her eyes well with tears. She touched his face gently and turned around. She rushed out of the apartment. She didn't take the lift. She didn't want to hang around a minute longer. As she went down four lots of stairs, she couldn't stop her tears. She only wiped them when she left the building. She walked for hours. She saw people, lovers holding hands, dog owners and their pets, children playing in the parks, cars honking, long-distance trucks arriving in Paris with goods for the week ahead. Her feet were heavy and aching. She finally found a bench at the edge of a park and sat down. Why was she like this? Why couldn't she truly fall in love with anyone? She thought of herself as a person with a serious disability – one that could not be seen by anyone looking at her. And then she heard herself say, 'Damn you, Tony...'

CHAPTER 15

THE ROAD TO DAMASCUS

Summer 1976

Heavy fighting in the vicinity of the airport and the constant shelling had prevented planes from taking off and landing at Beirut International Airport. It remained closed for the time being. And no one knew for certain when it would reopen. After Tony and Nora's return to East Beirut, they had begun earnestly to prepare for their departure for Paris. Waleed and Carole were supposed to be doing the same in West Beirut. All four were not sure whether they'd be able to fly out of Beirut. During this time, the Beirut Museum Green Line crossing had been reopened for cars and Tony told Nora that he would be crossing over to West Beirut for a few days on his own. When Nora asked him why she couldn't join him, he said he needed to go to help Waleed with the selling of his car. He didn't give her any further details, which she found strange. 'All boring stuff for you', was all Tony said. He called her the day after his departure to West Beirut from Waleed's apartment. He sounded agitated and his voice was full of angst and urgency.

"We've got to leave in the next few days," he told her. "And Waleed is coming to East Beirut with me. His suitcase is already packed."

"What about Carole? Isn't she coming too?"

"No. She's busy with her sister who's just got married and is leaving for Australia in the next few days. Ramzi promised he'll drive her to the Green Line and we'll pick her up from there when we're ready to depart. I called you to expressly ask you to be ready to depart in three or four days. You need to talk to your parents today."

"Why are you in such a hurry to leave, Tony?"

"I'm telling you we've got to leave as soon as possible!"

"Why are you yelling, Tony! That's so unlike you."

"I apologize – I'm just worried we might get stuck here and not be able to leave at all. The Airport's still closed as you know. The only way out of here is through the Damascus Highway. I'm just afraid they may close that too."

"Okay, don't worry too much. I'll talk to my parents tonight. I'll tell them that we'll be going to Syria and flying out of Damascus. Let's keep our fingers crossed."

Nora's father accepted the reasoning that even the Damascus Highway might be in danger of closing and gave his permission for Nora to leave as quickly as possible. He gave her a good sum of money, too. Even though he now had no work, he said he'd divided the money he had into four – the number corresponding to the number of family members. The money he was giving her was her share.

"But Dad, that's too much money!" she protested. "I'll get part-time work when I get to Paris."

"That's not too much money for Paris," he said. "Just make sure you hide it well during the journey. And forget the part-time work for now and concentrate on your studies there. This money should see you through for a year. After that, God will help us and I hope I can start working again and send you more money."

"But Dad..."

"All I want you to do is to complete your studies in France. The future is bleak for all of us here. I'd be more than satisfied if one of us can get out of this hell hole."

Nora was so touched by her father's gesture that she swore she would find part-time work when she got to Paris to support herself as a student. Other than the initial expenses and travelling costs, she vowed to keep the money he had given her intact and return it to him the following year. The moment she got to Paris, she'd open a bank account and keep the money safe there. And as she'd vowed, she did return it to him a year later when she went back to Beirut to visit her parents. By then, although her father was working, his earnings never again matched those of his pre-civil war ones. He would not admit it because of his pride, but her family was always short of funds. Her father died four years later, followed by her mother who could not accept living life without him. Nora was certain that their premature deaths were a direct cause of the blows of the civil war they had to deal with. Their lifestyle was not the same as it was in the past and it could never be righted.

Nora left Beirut with Tony, Carole and Waleed three days later. Before their departure, the three, who were in East Beirut, met up with Carole at a location near the Green Line. And the last person they said a sad goodbye to was Ramzi who had driven Carole over to the meeting point. Sana was not with him but she had sent them a goodbye note. The four of them then hired a taxi to take them to Damascus International Airport. As soon as they got on the Damascus Highway, Carole said, 'This is our road to Damascus – just like Saul in the Bible, who became Saint Paul, we're saved!' She looked at Nora, Tony, and Waleed, and smiled. Nora felt her heart bursting with joy. She was sitting next to Tony and she leaned towards him and placed her head on his shoulder. This is how they travelled on the plane that took them to Paris, too. Nora felt serene and secure with him. It finally dawned on her that Tony was the most important person in her life. And that she loved him.

Paris was already full of acquaintances from Beirut. The four of them were not the only ones who had thought of seeking refuge in France. Many young people had left Beirut earlier than they did and had settled in the city in a short period. Phone calls to some of these acquaintances had secured them accommodation in an expensive city. Like true refugees, everybody helped newcomers with tips about how to go about living in Paris. Tony and Waleed found free lodging with a schoolmate of Waleed's who had been there for six months and was already employed as a bartender. Nora and Carole got free temporary use of a studio flat which belonged to one of Nora's brother's friends, a French Armenian who had bought the studio as an investment flat.

Their timing was good, too. They had arrived in July – perfect timing to begin student university enrolment procedures. They soon met others like them – young Lebanese students, who guided them through the steps of dealing with daily life in the city. When students from a war-torn country meet somewhere else in the world, there is always camaraderie and an urge to help each other. Under normal circumstances, this may not always be the case. Thus, they first received guidance in how to register for a university enrolment. Nora couldn't believe how easy this was. All they had to do was present their high school papers, university transcripts, and pay the registration fee. There were no tuition fees to pay – universities were free in Paris. Once they'd done this, they had to obtain a residence permit. Although the Paris Prefecture followed the usual tedious French bureaucracy, the residence permits were obtained with no hiccups. The French, because of their historical ties with Lebanon, had adopted a policy of facilitating the stay of Lebanese nationals on their territory.

In a couple of weeks, Nora, Tony, Carole and Waleed, had learned how to use the Paris Metro, where to purchase the cheapest priced foods, which cafes offered the cheapest coffee, where to go for a Lebanese meal if they missed it, and most important, how to make a free phone call to Lebanon. This they learned from others like them. International phone calls from Paris were very expensive. They had to call their families to reassure them that they were doing well. Once a week, they'd go to an area of Paris that was not centrally located, like Belleville, in the evening. They'd roam the streets until they could spot a public phone booth that had a long queue in front of it – an indication it was a 'free' phone call booth. The trick was to use a used yellow metro ticket which was hard enough to jam the receiver's mechanism. This allowed for making international phone calls without having to put coins in the machine. Once someone had jammed the phone, it was then free for everyone waiting in the queue. Yes, it was illegal to do this, but they'd join the queue and wait for hours for their turn – sometimes until the small hours of the morning even when it was freezing cold in the months that followed. They'd now and again spot a police car patrolling the area, but no one was bothered about it. The police obviously knew what they were up to and turned a blind eye to the activity.

Everything seemed to be going well for them except for Waleed's melancholy and lack of enthusiasm when they planned any kind of activity. Both Nora and Carole had noticed that since the day they left Beirut, he wasn't his usual self.

"What's wrong with Waleed?" asked Nora.

"You've noticed, have you?" Carole responded. "I wanted to mention it to you. I really don't know why he looks so depressed. We're doing fine in Paris. I try to cheer him up. And when I ask him if something's wrong, he just doesn't say anything. He's gone back to his extreme introvert-self mode. He's like when I first met him. I really don't know what to do anymore. I'm really worried about him."

"I wonder why this sudden reversal and why when we're in Paris? How is he treating you?"

"I can't complain. He's even more tender and affectionate than he ever was with me when we're on our own. It's just that I feel he's drowning in melancholy and I can't explain it."

"I'll talk to Tony. Maybe he knows something," Nora said.

"Oh, would you? Maybe Tony knows what's bothering Waleed."

When Nora mentioned Waleed's behaviour to Tony and asked if Tony knew why Waleed permanently looked so sad, he just ignored her question. But Nora wouldn't let go and asked another question.

"Is he depressed because he doesn't have access to hasheesh like he used to in Beirut?"

"Stop asking me questions like that, Nora!"

"Why are you so agitated? I'm just worried about Waleed."

"Stop putting your nose into things that don't concern you!"

"What?! Waleed is my friend, too. I have the right to ask. You should know better."

"Well, I don't know. Stop it! You don't have to know everything, Nora."

This was the first ever argument they were having. Nora was taken aback. What was he hiding?

"You're lying to me. You're hiding something. I feel it."

"Please, Nora. Drop it!"

"I'm not going to! Is he depressed because he can't get hold of hasheesh?"

No reply came from Tony. He just threw himself on the tiny sofa in the studio where she was staying, and then hid his face with his hands. Nora went and sat next to him, and she began massaging his back.

"Why are we arguing like this? We've never argued before. Tony, look at me. What's happening?"

Tony now looked at her.

"He does have access to hasheesh," he said quietly, holding her hand.

"How?"

"He brought some with him from Lebanon."

"What?! You mean he brought hasheesh on the flight?"

"Yes. Don't be upset. I was going to tell you eventually."

"How did he do that? Where did he hide it?"

"You know the hard cover English literature book that we all used in high school – he removed the paper stuck on the inside part of the hard covers. He flattened the hasheesh and hid it on each side and then re-glued the paper sheets."

"I can't believe what you're telling me!" Nora said, shocked. "We could have all been arrested if he'd been caught at the airport. The four of us were travelling together, for Heaven's sake!"

Nora let go of his hand.

"I know. I'm sorry. It was better if you and Carole didn't know."

"I'm really disappointed in you. You went along with it."

"Don't blame me, Nora. You're happy to jam phones and cheat the Paris Municipality just so you can talk to your parents for free and that's okay, but this isn't?"

"I admit both behaviours are condemnable. But this could have landed us in jail in France, Tony."

"Listen, Nora, Waleed is going through a hard patch at the moment. He was on the verge of having a nervous breakdown just before we left Beirut. That's why I went to see him on my own before we left Beirut. I couldn't tell you because he asked me not to. Do you understand?"

"Nonsense! Why? I thought he was happy. He's got Carole."

"I think her abortion affected him greatly. You know he's psychologically very fragile. In rational terms, he understood it and forgave Carole, but it still had an impact on him psychologically. I mean he can't help it. He's a lot weaker than Carole in that sense. And..."

"And what?"

"Nothing!"

"So, you didn't talk him out of bringing hasheesh with him to France because of that?"

"I admit I'm guilty. I didn't. I thought it would help in calming his nerves."

"And has it worked?"

"He's fine at night when he's smoking. I think he'll be fine given time."

"At night? You mean he's not okay during the day because he's not smoking his hasheesh? What kind of logic is that?"

"Don't twist things, Nora. He's really depressed. He'll get over it – that's what he told me. He just needs some time. The hasheesh will help him get over his melancholy."

"What he needs is not hasheesh. He needs proper psychological treatment!"

Tony seemed agitated again. He got up and walked towards the window. He spoke to her without turning around, without looking at her face.

"Everything will be alright, Nora. Just let it be. I beg of you," he said.

Nora came over and gave him a back hug.

"What am I going to tell Carole? She's worried sick about him."

"Please tell her it's a phase that will pass. She's used to his melancholy. It's not the first time she's seen him like this. Let's not argue anymore, Nora," he said in a whisper.

"Okay," she said, letting go of him. "Now turn around and look at me."

Tony obeyed her. He slowly turned around to face her. His eyes told her to forgive him. He looked like a helpless boy whose mother had just scolded him for being naughty. She felt the urge and hugged him tightly.

"I'm sorry, I'm so sorry," he whispered in her ear.

She pushed him gently away, tip-toed to reach his height, and cupped his cheeks with both hands. Looking deep into his eyes, she brought her face close to his. She closed her eyes and gave him a kiss on the lips. He kissed her back softly – once, twice, three times and smiled.

"You're my girl," he said, and with all the strength he could muster, he carried her in his arms.

"Put me down, Tony, I'm too heavy!" she protested.

He laughed and sat her on the tiny sofa. He sat next to her. He stroked her hair and then kissed her again. Their gentle kiss turned into a passionate embrace. How long it lasted, Nora could not remember afterwards. All she knew was that it was their first one. It struck them both like a thunderbolt.

CHAPTER 16
THE CITY OF LIGHTS AND LOVE

Nora always remembered her first morning in Paris with nostalgia. Carole was making coffee when she opened her eyes. She got up quickly and practically flew to the only, very large, window in the studio, to open it. She breathed in the fresh air of the morning. So, this is what Paris felt like. The smell of the air was different from that of Beirut, but she liked it. The window was positioned at the back of the building and overlooked a courtyard. The courtyard was rectangular in shape. Two other buildings on the other side of theirs overlooked it, too. Nora, now leaning over the window sill, looked straight down and saw the concierge lady cleaning the courtyard while talking to someone. She couldn't see who the other person was, but the spoken French was pleasing to her ears. She felt so much joy at that moment. She would never forget that feeling. She had already fallen in love with Paris like one would fall in love at first sight.

The studio she shared with Carole was only 20 square metres but it had all the amenities. A kitchenette and a small bathroom were adequate for their needs. They were both grateful that the toilet was not on the landing, like it was where Waleed and Tony were staying, even though the building dated from the early 20th Century. It had a rickety, old elevator with a wrought iron door. It looked charmingly Parisian, but both Nora and Carole were afraid to use it. They preferred to take the stairs. Nora loved going up the old wooden stairs – so unlike the stone or cement ones in Beirut. The wooden stairs were caramel coloured and Nora found they gave a lived-in and warm atmosphere to the building. She found the old smell of the interior of the building and the old wooden doors with brass knobs on each floor, exotic. The one room that they had was tastefully decorated with a tiny sofa, a small table with four chairs, and a bookcase. The bed, which they shared, was suspended. They accessed it via a small wooden ladder at one corner of the room.

The studio, which they had free use of for a couple of months, was in Alésia, in the 14th Arrondissement. At the time, it was a mixed neighbourhood with well-to-do middle-class folks, students, and immigrants. Some parts of it felt bohemian and others modern with new buildings. Small shops, selling handicrafts, stood next to cheap clothing shops run by North African immigrants. The neighbourhood where Waleed and Tony stayed was very different. In the Pyrénées area of the 19th Arrondissement, their building was run down like most buildings in the vicinity and had not seen any loving care for decades. There was no shopping area – just greengrocers and a few old cheap cafes, frequented mainly by men. The inhabitants were poor folk, African and North African immigrants, and some students. For lack of space in Waleed's friend's studio, Waleed and Tony slept on the floor using old mattresses and sleeping bags. Waleed could have asked his parents to pay for his accommodation at a decent hotel. But he said he hated being on his own and preferred to rough it with Tony.

All four knew they had to find permanent accommo-dation for themselves once university started in October. Everyone they spoke to said that renting an apartment as students was out of the question. No one in Paris would rent a flat to a student normally for fear of non-payment and even if they did, the rent would be exorbitant. Rent-ing outside of Paris may have been possible but it would have meant long commuting journeys. The best option was to secure student accommodation at the Cité Universitaire, the student housing campus. It was July when they got to Paris and this could not be done before September. They had two months before they needed to deal with accom-modation and other university matters. They thus devoted their time to exploring Paris.

The Eiffel Tower, the Tuileries and Luxembourg gar-dens, the Champs Elysées, the Paris Opera, and the Lou-vre were the first places they visited like tourists but soon discovered the real treasures of the city. They were in awe of the architecture and exquisite décor of the 19th Century Paris passages, covered up-market passages where exclu-sive boutiques were housed. They had the same admiration when they set foot in the historic department store of the Bon Marché, the first department store in the world to have opened in 1852. Nearby, strolling up and down Rue du Bac and Rue du Four, they discovered the latest designs – from furniture to glasses. St. Germain des Près, with its famous cafes where French intellectuals used to hang out, fascinated them and so did all the side streets off the main drag, where antique shops and rare book sellers were plentiful.

As students, they could not afford any of the expensive items that they saw in the boutiques. Using a French phrase, they told each other they were doing 'lèche vitrine', literally 'licking the shop windows', which meant they were satisfied by just looking at the beautiful things they saw without the need for buying them. Affordable, trendy clothing, shoes, and accessories they quickly discovered could be found in the bohemian and student neighbourhoods of the city and in particular in the Censier area with its small boutiques where a vast selection of young or student fashion could be found and where tourists didn't venture. The young Lebanese who had got to Paris before them advised them to invest in warm overcoats for the Paris winter and comfortable pairs of shoes which they needed for the long walking distances both in the Paris Metro and the city in general.

Saint Michel was their preferred area, same as for any student or person of their age. It covered a large area from the Luxembourg Gardens all the way down to the Notre Dame Cathedral. For them, the main attraction was the large number of small bookshops where second-hand books of every sort could be had for peanuts. The famous English-language bookstore was one of their regular stops. There were countless music stores as well as cheap ethnic eateries in the narrow medieval streets off the main boulevard. It was at one of these eateries that they had their first taste of North African food. Sometimes they'd share a cheap couscous or have 'mergez' sausages and then colourful Moroccan sweets, other times they'd buy North African 'bambanya', a type of sandwich made with a huge bun, the size of two hamburgers, stuffed with tuna and pickles. It was also in the Saint Michel area that the small independent cinemas, with no more than 50 or so seats, were located and they could watch art house movies for a derisory price. And the choice of movies was mind-boggling. They could watch not only French movies but also a good number of African, North African, and Latin American films as well.

Paris was not always the epitome of glamour and beautiful things. There was the seedy Paris, too. All four of them were shocked to see half-clad prostitutes openly accosting potential customers on a street in the centre of town, not far from Les Halles. On another occasion, they went to explore the Montmartre area, high up the hill. When it got dark, they walked back down the narrow roads and found themselves in the middle of Pigalle where the seedy night clubs of Paris were in full swing. They passed in front of well-lit sex shops and peep show kiosks. And then they spotted a group of very tall and slim ladies. They were clad in sequined tight dresses and had long, blond hair wigs on. Their faces were masked with thick layers of makeup. They walked in their red or gold stiletto high heels with natural ease – as if they were born in them. As they got closer to the group, the four of them could hear them talking and giggling but their voice pitch was not one that they associated with females. Then the penny dropped – they were transgenders or transvestites. Not one of the four could tell which they were.

Experiencing Paris without including its culinary delights is a true sign of failure. Thus, the four of them embarked on discovering those that were not already familiar to them. They all knew what a baguette was, but there were so many other kinds of bread in the Paris bakeries. The 'ficelle', a very thin baguette, and the 'pain', thicker than a baguette were a regular component of a baker's repertoire. 'Rilletes', shredded pork preserved in fat, and the French saucisson, hung-dried meat, were a novelty and became Nora's and Tony's favourites as they often had them for dinner instead of a cooked meal. All four loved the Parisian handmade ice cream and sorbets with their myriad of flavours and some unusual types like the chocolate sorbet. And then there were the enticing patisseries with their mouth-watering cakes unmatched anywhere else in the world. It was true that they could not afford to dine in fancy restaurants where well-known chefs operated, but simple food was as exciting to them as Michelin-starred menus. They discovered this was what the local French people felt like too; they appreciated a slice of country ham in a buttered half a baguette from their local café, or a steak frites (steak and French fries) at a local eatery perhaps more than sophisticated meals.

Even before starting university, they'd begun frequenting the subsidized student university restaurants. The one hot meal of the day they chose to have at one of these restaurants. They'd buy the restaurant vouchers from university students who had the habit of buying them in sets of ten. At 3.50 French Francs per meal, they were the cheapest in Paris. They were nothing like the chef-prepared fine French cuisine dishes. They were basic cafeteria-type food, but the menu included a large selection because these restaurants catered for thousands of students each day. They even had couscous, the North African stew with couscous grains. This was extremely popular with students and on the menu on Wednesdays, the only day that students were willing to queue for their meal.

On certain days, the menu included local fish and 'boudin', the French black pudding. One time, Tony insisted that Nora try a big meat ball which she hadn't seen before. He grabbed the plate from the display counter and placed it on her tray. She enquired as to what it was. He said he'd tell her once she had the first mouthful. She cut into the large meat ball, twice the size of a tennis ball, and discovered it was made up of a stringy type of meat. She had her first mouthful and told Tony it was delicious. It was then that Tony divulged it was horse meat. She had eaten French snails in Lebanon many times as she was growing up. But she was shocked at what she had just consumed. Tony assured her that horse meat was very popular in France. He told her butchers only sold the meat of old horses which were at the last stages of their lives. She wasn't sure he was telling her the truth, but she had already told him she liked the taste of it, so she couldn't take back her words.

With the exception of Waleed, there was one French dessert that the three of them could not resist having. It was called a 'Liègeoise'. They never understood why it had a Belgian name. They did not go to the Galleries Lafayette, the biggest department store in the city, to do their shopping like other people did. They specifically went there to have this dessert which was served at the top floor café at a knock-down price. All three had grown up loving Chantilly cream on cakes or desserts in Lebanon. But the 'Liègeoise' offered them much more than just a bit of Chantilly cream. It was in fact a big, tall glass of Chantilly cream all on its own – a pure delight!

━┉╋┉━

Two weeks after their arrival in Paris, both Waleed and Tony complained that they were having a hard time washing. There was no shower or bathtub in the studio where they were staying. The only way to wash was in the toilet cubicle on the landing which had a squat WC. They would have to fill the large bucket that was at one corner of it and scoop the water with a large, ladle-like contraption. When Nora and Carole heard about this, they convinced the boys that they should come over and have their baths at their place. Thus, Tony and Waleed began turning up at the girls' studio every other day and took turns to take a shower or a bath. They'd have a meal together, then they'd get carried away talking until very late at night and the boys would miss the last metro. Inevitably, Waleed and Tony would sleep over. Eventually, Tony and Waleed decided to remedy the situation by buying two mattresses. They slept on the floor, while the girls slept in the suspended bed.

As days passed, the four of them practically started living together in the Alésia studio. But the sleeping arrangement changed. Carole ended up sleeping on the mattress with Waleed and Tony ended up sleeping in the same suspended bed as Nora. It happened one day when Tony turned up at the studio on his own in the evening. Carole had gone out to meet Waleed at a bookshop and Nora was alone in the studio. Tony took his usual shower. When he came out with only a towel wrapped over the lower part of his body and his naked torso showing, Nora was overcome by a fierce desire to hold him and kiss him. He must have read her thoughts. He approached her and gently kissed her on her lips. She responded and then held him close to her. She covered his naked shoulder with quick kisses. 'Let's go to bed', he said and pulled her by the hand.

They lay side by side on the suspended bed. He slowly undressed her. She felt so shy that she covered her private parts with her arms and hands. 'Let go', he ordered her and pushed her hands away. He kissed her, thrusting his tongue deep into her mouth. He then pulled her close to him. Her nipples touched his chest. He felt their softness on his skin. He kissed her on the neck now and gently pushing her away from him, started to kiss her breasts. He took her nipples one by one and sucked on them slowly. He then reached for her private part and gently touched it with his finger until her juices started flowing. 'I don't think I'm ready yet to go all the way', she whispered in his ear. 'I know', he said now looking deep into her eyes. He then directed her hand toward the lower part of his torso. 'I'll show you how to do it', he said. She complied. When he came, his head fell back on the pillow. 'You're my one and only Nora', he said, pulling her over and resting her head on his chest.

Waleed and Carole turned up at that precise moment. Finding them in the suspended bed, Waleed said they'd be going out for a meal and quickly left with Carole to give them the privacy they needed. They returned very late at night and didn't bother them. Tony and Nora had already made the suspended bed their own cocoon. They spent that first night in silence. They explored each other's bodies and showered them with caresses and kisses in the darkness. They could not have had this freedom to discover each other in Beirut. Their emotions were unbridled. And this is what the City of Love had in store for them. Their hearts were filled with a kind of joy neither of them had experienced before. But even though they both felt the same way about each other, neither of them had the courage to express the words 'I love you'.

CHAPTER 17
I HAVE SOMETHING
IMPORTANT TO TELL YOU

Autumn 2015

'There – your double espresso,' Tony said and placed the coffee on the corner table at the café he had taken Nora to in Toronto. Nora watched the movement of his arms and when he sat down, she looked at his face. Was she really living this moment? It was too surreal. Life was full of surprises. How could she be sitting opposite him after all those years? He hadn't changed much – his face still had a youthful look save for a few wrinkles here and there. He was the only man she had loved all her life. She had known it years ago. Now that she was able to talk to him, sitting so close to him, did she feel she still loved him? Presently, she felt she should stop herself from analysing her feelings. This was not the purpose of her visit.

Surprisingly, the café was almost empty with only two tables occupied at the opposite end of where they were. Tony welcomed the quiet as he had planned to have a long conversation with Nora before they headed to Hamilton.

"So, tell me about your life, Nora. We have a lot of catching up to do," he began.

"Two failed relationships and no marriage," she said with a sarcastic tone. "But I have a beautiful daughter and we get on very well. We're like close friends – although sometimes she can be frustrating when she behaves like a true millennial," and laughed.

"I know what you mean. I could say the same thing about Paul," he said with a smile.

"She's going to be 35 soon! She's a fashion executive in Paris – loves her job. And she's engaged to a really nice guy. In fact, she's pregnant and they'll be getting married in a few months."

"Congratulations! You must be very proud of her. And you must be thrilled – you're going to be a grandmother!"

"I am. But don't remind me of the grandmother part..." she said, rolling her eyes. "What about Paul?"

"Paul is doing alright. He teaches music at one of the universities here and goes to New York quite often for music production jobs when they happen. He was musically very gifted as a child. We made every effort to get him accepted at the famous Berklee College of Music in Boston where he graduated from with flying colours. He's not one to settle down with a permanent relationship though. He's had countless girlfriends but none serious enough, I guess," he said and then added, "My job here at the aluminium company is for life, so I have no complaints. How about you? Are you still working for the same PR company?"

"Yes, I am, but I think my days there are numbered even though I have a management position now. Quite a few people have been let go of in the lower echelons of the company already. From what I hear, the executive board will announce further cuts in the coming year. I felt quite safe until now, especially after I headed the team for a very important contract in Dubai last winter. I spent three months there. But now I'm not so sure."

"Surely, they need all your expertise and your knowledge of so many languages."

"Perhaps – but they will fire the older employees first. How's your sister and her family?" she said to change the subject.

"Oh, she's fine. She had three kids in quick succession when she first got here. They are all married with their own families now. Did you know that it was because of her that we ended up in Canada? I mean she vouched for me and Carole and that's how we landed here as legal immigrants."

"Yeah – I remember. By the way, did you know that Sana now lives in Abu Dhabi? We met once in Dubai when I was working there."

"No, I didn't. How is she? Is she married? Tell me about her! I often think of Ramzi and it upsets me every time…"

"She's married. She has four children." Nora paused. "Can we talk about this another time, Tony? It's too painful for me, too. I'll eventually tell you about my encounter with her. I will – there's only the four of us now left in this world…"

"So true. And we will lose Carole, too…" he said, lowering his head. There was a long silence and Nora didn't know what to say. "Even after all these years, I think about Waleed, Ramzi, and Michel almost every day of my life," he re-started the conversation.

"I'll tell you something that will make you happy, I'm sure," she said to counter the sadness that was written all over Tony's face. "A few weeks before Michel went to do his military service, he called me and asked to meet me at a café near my house. He said he wanted to share with me an experience he'd had. He was too shy to tell you about it."

"Really? Why?"

"Well, he just wanted to tell me about his love life – I mean, you know how it is with young girls telling each other about boyfriends and Michel wanted to do the same, you understand? He was so excited that he wanted to tell someone about his boyfriend. Did he mention to you a young man who worked at the bookshop near his school?"

"Yes, he did, briefly. I do remember him saying he was attracted to him, that's all."

"Well, Michel met him one evening at closing time. They went for a drink and Michel ended up at the guy's apartment. I think his name was Sami if my memory serves me right. Michel had his first and only true love affair and sexual encounter with him. I saw that Sami at Michel's funeral. Although I didn't know him personally, I guessed it was him. He fit the description Michel had given me. He was crying the whole time and wore a silver chain bracelet that Michel had told me he'd given him as a token of their love before joining the army."

Nora noticed Tony's eyes watering, but he quickly gave her a smile.

"Thanks for telling me this after all these years. Michel is the one I miss most to tell you the truth – he was my closest buddy and could never be replaced. I've made very few friends here, like our next-door neighbours, but it's not the same. It makes me feel better to know that my best friend tasted the pleasures of love before he died." A long silence followed yet again.

"Have you been to Beirut since immigrating to Canada?"

"I went twice for my parents' funerals quite a few years ago now. I had no reason to go back there after that. My eldest sister is here and the younger one lives in California. I saw her last year. She came for Christmas. Carole never went back to Beirut. Her older sister and parents immigrated to Australia right after Paul was born and that's where her parents passed away. She contacts her sister quite regularly by phone. And you?" he inquired.

"I've been four times since I settled in Paris. Twice I took my daughter there so she could spend time with her grandparents. My parents were over the moon, of course. They spoiled her rotten like all grandparents do. The other times were to attend my parents' funerals. I still miss them so much," she said and covered her eyes with one hand. She re-composed herself a few minutes later. "There's no one of my nearest and dearest left in Beirut. They all left as years went by. My brother lives in Thailand now, so we don't see each other as often as we wish."

"That's our lot," he said, "and the civil war destroyed our happy lives in Lebanon. After my parents died, nothing urged me to go back. It's sad to go back when none of the people we were close to are there, my immediate family included. Michel's mother is still alive and she lives with her daughter in Kuwait. Practically all the people we knew then are scattered around the world now."

"True," she responded and looked at his kind face. He looked into her eyes with his affectionate gaze and then, embarrassed, looked away and said:

"Nora, I've booked a room for you in a hotel in the downtown area of Hamilton, near the hospital."

"Thanks, Tony."

"But before we leave, I have something important to tell you."

"I'm all ears," she said wondering what it was that was so important.

"You're going to meet Paul at the hospital when we get there. We take turns and he's there now because I needed to pick you up. It's not easy for me to say this," he said lowering his voice. "I don't want you to be shocked when you see him. I knew I had to have the guts to tell you this before you saw him."

"He's not handicapped or anything like that – is he? You never sent me his pictures as a baby."

"No, no. It's nothing like that. He's a very healthy young man."

"Then what is it?"

"He looks exactly like Waleed."

There was yet another long silence. Nora was computing in her head what she'd just heard. Did she hear that right? She felt her face getting all hot and red. She closed her eyes for a moment.

"Are you saying Paul is Waleed's child?"

"Yes," Tony said in a whisper.

"So, Carole was pregnant with Waleed's child when you married her?"

"Yes, she was."

"And you kept this from me for all these years," she said in an accusatory tone.

"I owe you an apology. But at the time, we agreed not to tell anyone that Paul was Waleed's child. With Waleed gone, there was no point in complicating things, especially for our parents."

"I get it and your apology is accepted," she said, not knowing what else to say.

The two of them continued drinking their coffees without saying anything to each other and without making eye contact.

"You never loved me, not even then," she eventually blurted out, surprised at her outburst, and couldn't stop the flow of her tears.

"Don't do this, Nora," Tony said, and reaching across the table, cupped her hand with his. His gesture made her cry even more.

"You never really cared about me, Tony," she said, wiping her tears with the end of her paper tissue.

"I did and I always have."

"That's the biggest lie I've ever heard. You never even asked about me or showed any compassion all these years. You completely forgot the affection we had for each other – even as friends."

"I do care about you. I always have and always will – why would I have checked on you otherwise?" He said, defiantly.

Was this a slip of the tongue? Nora wasn't sure.

"What do you mean checking on me?"

"I always asked to be sent to Paris for work assignments," he said rubbing his head. "I went there six times over the last 25 years. And each time, I did check on you to make sure you were alright. I never contacted you. I didn't feel I had the right to. I didn't want to interfere with your life. Each time I was there, I followed you home from work but you were never aware of my presence. One morning, I saw you taking your daughter to school. That was the first time I saw you after I left for Canada. The last time, seven years ago, I followed you on one of your shopping sprees."

"You were spying on me. I'm gob-smacked," she said, opening her eyes wider.

"Come on, Nora – if you want to put it that way, I can't negate that."

"It's not fair. That's why you were quick at recognizing me at the airport. Not fair at all on me – leaving me in the dark about all of this like I was some sort of an insignificant mushroom."

"I couldn't see you or set up a meeting to explain things. Only now I can do it. Please forgive me – a thousand apologies."

Seeing him sad, she weakened and softened.

"Did you really love Carole to marry her, Tony?"

"I grew fond of her," was Tony's prompt reply.

Nora didn't wish to pursue the matter any further. She felt uneasy.

"Does Paul know he's Waleed's son?"

"He doesn't."

That was another bit of information that shook Nora to the core.

"I mean, I planned to tell him when he was old enough but Carole stopped me. I don't look anything like him I told her. She said Paul didn't know any of her relatives and assumed he'd taken the physical traits of her side of the family. There's not much difference between the way that Waleed looked, with his olive skin and curly hair, and a certain type of Jewish male – is there?"

Nora didn't answer that question and looked at Tony's face, astounded.

"What I don't understand is why Carole doesn't want Paul to know Waleed is his father. It's puzzling."

"You need to ask Carole that directly," he said and looked inside the now empty cup of coffee in front of him, somewhat agitated.

"I shall not mention Waleed in Paul's presence – I got that – rest assured," she said with a smile, wanting to finish the conversation on a positive note.

Taking the cue from her, Tony said, "Shall we head for Hamilton then?"

As they walked towards the car in silence, Tony felt a huge burden taken off his shoulders. He was satisfied that he was finally able to tell Nora that Paul was Waleed's son. Nora, on the other hand, felt turmoil building up in her heart. She was surprised at how easily she and Tony could converse even though their discussion included the divulging of an important secret. It was as if the 38-year gap between the last time they spoke to each other properly and the present time had vanished into thin air. She was flattered and elated that he'd specifically asked to be assigned to come to Paris to make sure she was alive and well. But she could sense there was still an invisible barrier between him and her. She didn't know why or what it was, but it was certainly there. What other secrets was he keeping from her? When she fell in love with him all those years ago, she was certain he looked up to her and was loyal to her. She thought she knew him so well then. She thought she could read him, his thoughts. Even now, she couldn't believe he could have had a change of heart about their relationship merely for the sake of protecting Carole because she was pregnant with Waleed's child. And what did he mean when he said he grew fond of Carole after he married her? Was he lying to her when he wrote to her and said he'd fallen in love with Carole? Was he lying to her then or was he lying to her now?

"I have a headache coming on," she said in the car after Tony had started driving.

"I have Tylenol in the glove compartment if you want to take one."

"Sure. I guess it's the long flight," she said.

"Nora, I'm sorry. What I said and this trip is going to be quite stressful for you, but Carole wants desperately to see you for one last time."

"Stop apologizing, Tony. I understand and I'm here because I want to be."

"Don't ever doubt my affection for you," he said after a while, without glancing at her but looking at the road ahead.

CHAPTER 18
THE VANISHING POINT

Summer 1978

Ramzi put his best clothes on. He had a date with Sana that evening and they were to meet at their usual haunt. He brushed his wavy hair and thought about his friends. How he missed them and the old times. It had nearly been two years since they had left for Paris. Even with the tragic demise of Waleed, he had envied the others and many of his acquaintances for having left Lebanon for new horizons. 'I owe you big time', the last words that Waleed told him before he left for Paris came to his mind. 'You don't owe me anything, buddy', he said to himself and tried to put the tragedy out of his mind.

No, he wasn't jealous of people for having left Lebanon. He wasn't like that. He wished them well and hoped with all his heart that they would have a happy life wherever they went. If only he and Sana were able to leave when the others left, they would be married by now. They'd be somewhere where they had freedom – somewhere without any of the constraints placed on them in Lebanon. Still, he thought he had done well for himself. As one of the bodyguards of the Imam, he had saved a considerable amount of money over the last two years. He had never imagined he would be able to make that much in such a short period. He wanted someone to pat him on the shoulder and thought the day to marry Sana was nearing. With universities re-opening shortly after his friends left Beirut, Sana was able to continue her studies and would soon be able to finish her nursing degree. That would be a good time to finally make her his wife. The anticipation of their big day approaching filled his heart with immense joy. He dearly wished it to happen without too much difficulty.

Sana was already waiting for him when he got to Abu Ali's place. She was sitting at their usual table. She was wearing a black dress with a red flower brooch pinned on the left side of her chest.

"You look beautiful!" he said and gave her a red rose that he had picked up on the way.

She thanked him and kissed him on the cheek.

"This is the 40th rose you've given me. I counted them yesterday. I never throw them away as you know. I keep each one in one of my books when they dry out."

He nodded and gave her a kiss on her cheek and held her hand.

"What's your news?" he said as was his customary expression when starting their face-to-face conversations.

"I got a letter from Nora yesterday. It was delivered by someone who has recently returned from Paris," Sana began.

"Really? What did she say? Is everything okay with them? Good news I hope after that sad, sad story of Waleed's."

"Actually, it is puzzling news. I don't know what to make of it. Nora wrote that Tony married Carole and is taking her to Canada with him."

"What? What's going on? I thought Tony was in love with Nora. That's what he led me to understand. This is truly strange," he said, drawing back his upper body from her to express his utter surprise.

"Nora is of course devastated. She doesn't know how it happened either."

"I would categorize the behaviour as shameful if I didn't know Tony better," Ramzi responded. "I need to find a way of getting in touch with Tony to find out what really happened. It's frustrating not being able to get in touch with him easily. People change, I guess, and they do unexpected things. Sana, I don't understand it at all. I can never do that to you – not in a million years!"

There was a long silence. They were both trying to come to terms with what had happened between Tony and Nora and they could not find words to describe such an anomaly. Sana now took the rose she had placed on the table, looked at it and smelt it.

"You really spoil me, you know that? You make me so happy – sometimes I think I'm in a wonderful dream!"

"And I will make you happier, I promise. Sana, I can today tell you that I have enough money for us to start a family soon. As soon as you graduate, we'll get married. I can ask for your hand with my head held high," he said.

"And if my father still refused to give his consent?"

"I'll think of a way to convince him. Now I know many people in high places through the Imam. They can intervene on my behalf."

"Listen, Ramzi, I've been thinking a lot lately and want to tell you this. If nothing works and we can't get my father's consent, I am now ready to renounce being a Sunni. Previously, I was not certain, but now I am. I don't mind becoming a Shiite to marry you. Your people can protect us, won't they? And once we have our first child, I'm sure my parents would want to see their grandchild and all will be forgiven."

Ramzi was surprised at that statement but delighted to hear it at the same time.

"Let's hope you don't have to renounce anything for my sake," he said and kissed her hand. He then added, "I'm sorry to tell you this, but we won't be able to see each other for a couple of weeks. The Imam is scheduled to make several trips to different locations in Lebanon and then there's an official visit to Libya. I'll be busy and I won't know my exact timetable ahead of time for security reasons."

"I understand," she said and smiled.

"I'll contact you as usual once everything's over," he said and kissed her cheek again tenderly.

Ramzi served the Imam with true sincerity and with all his heart. He didn't think he'd admired anyone in his life as much as he did the Imam. A Shiite religious head who was of Persian origin and who had tirelessly worked for the Arab Shiite community's rights in Lebanon was worthy of reverence. The Imam was a wise man, too. He had established the Amal (Hope) Movement and given hope for a better future to Ramzi's Shiite community – the poorest of the communities in the country. And, although the Imam had indeed formed a militia group around the movement, he had refused to engage in the fighting that was raging in the country. His efforts in acting as a mediator between the two sides of the conflict to promote peace had been recognised by others outside Ramzi's community and beyond the borders of Lebanon. Nevertheless, the Imam's security was paramount in the minds of his entourage. They could not dismiss the likely existence of dark forces thriving on the conflict of hundreds of years between the Shiite and Sunni factions of Islam and the race to dominate the region.

Ramzi placed his revolver in its holster and wore his suit jacket. The Imam was ready to depart for Libya. Ramzi, with other bodyguards, followed the Imam, darting his eyes left to right, up and down. Once on board the plane, they were all relieved everything had gone smoothly without any hiccups and Ramzi and the others took their seats behind the Imam and the small group of his personal entourage. Soon afterwards, food was served and discussions about the trip followed in whispers with the Imam. It was apparent that this was an important trip for the Imam, judging by the serious tone in which advisers were talking to him. Ramzi was not privy to any of these conversations, but was certain the Imam would triumph in whatever he had set out to do in Libya.

Some of Ramzi's colleagues had dozed off a few hours after take-off. On assignments like these, Ramzi could never behave like they did even if he felt tired. He briefly closed his eyes and thought of Sana. There was no one in this world that he loved more than her. She was ever-present in his heart and mind. Every move he made was for her. And he felt overjoyed that they would soon be united in marriage. In fact, even though he felt happy that he was on the right track, his patience was running out. He had to marry her as soon as he got back from this trip.

Someone from the Imam's entourage loudly announced that they were nearing landing time. 'Another few weeks and Sana will be my wife', Ramzi thought as he readied himself, unaware of the bitter fate that was waiting for him.

⊷⊶

'The Imam and his entourage have gone missing on their trip to Libya'. The news was all over the TV channels and radio stations. Newspapers splashed it as their cover story.

When she first heard the news, Sana's heart sank and she thought she was going to faint. She tried hard to control her emotions and thought it must be a mistake. How can a group of people disappear just like that? She thought 'Ramzi will call me any minute now to tell me it's all a lie and he's fine'. She waited patiently for two days but no phone call came. On the third day, she had lost her patience and began to cry incessantly. She locked herself in her room and listened to all the radio stations she could think of. Nobody seemed to know what had happened to the Imam and his entourage. One thing all the media people were certain about was that neither the Imam nor members of his entourage could be reached, which meant they were missing. Political experts quickly offered their analyses. Some said their plane was blown up just before landing in Libya. Others were of the opinion that the Imam and his entourage were kidnapped the minute their plane landed and that a high ransom will be asked in exchange for their freedom. Yet others were more pessimistic and said that the Libyans killed them the minute the Imam's plane landed in their country. The reason given was that it was a regional Arab game. It was being played to weaken the rising importance of Shiite communities in a region dominated by Sunni powers.

Sana was beside herself. She felt helpless and alone. What could she do? She couldn't get in touch with Ramzi's family or his uncle; she didn't know where they lived exactly. She couldn't tell anyone in her family about it. All she could do was to believe in the theory that the Imam and his entourage were kidnapped and ransom would surely be paid to have them released. She cried and prayed to dear God that Ramzi would be spared and would return to her unharmed.

"Have you been crying? Why are your eyes so red and swollen?" Sana's mum said when she caught Sana sneaking out of her room to go to the washroom.

"It's nothing. I don't feel well. I have a headache," she said and not being able to hold back, burst into tears.

"What's going on, my darling daughter? Tell me – what is it?" her mum said and hugged her.

"I failed in two courses," Sana lied.

"Come now, you can retake the exams or repeat the courses, can't you? It will be alright. You'll pass the courses, I'm sure," she said, still hugging her and caressing her hair.

Her mother then released her and wiped her tears. She asked Sana to help her prepare dinner. Holding Sana's hand, she dragged her into the kitchen and began her usual chatter about this, that and the other.

For the first time in her life, Sana was glad to have lied to her mother. It gave her the excuse not to have to participate in family gatherings and be absent at eating times. The next day she overheard her father say, 'What's wrong with Sana? Why is she always locking herself up in her room?' Her mother replied, 'She's studying for exam re-sits. The poor thing failed the first time around. So let her get on with it. Let her be, will you?'

Days, weeks, and months passed with no word from Ramzi. Sana resumed her normal life. She had to – she couldn't possibly remain in her bedroom forever and she needed to get out of the house for a bit of freedom and maybe to do something to find Ramzi. The only person Sana could confide in was a new friend she'd made at nursing school, Fatima. Fatima had replaced Carole in covering up for Sana when she went on dates with Ramzi. She had never met Ramzi in person and didn't know much about him, but was aware of how serious their relationship was.

"Why aren't you contacting Ramzi's parents or his uncle? They probably know a lot more than you do," Fatima told Sana.

"I've thought about it all these past months, but I don't actually know their home addresses. I could possibly find out, but what am I going to tell them if I do visit them? Tell them I'm his girlfriend? They don't know about me. I'd asked Ramzi not to tell them until we were ready to get married. And it would be too painful. I can't bear his mother crying. It will destroy me."

"What else can we do?" Fatima inquired.

"The only way of finding anything out is to go to the Imam's headquarters in the southern suburbs. It's really a daunting task for two Sunni girls to venture there, but will you come with me?"

"I'm ready to go, for your sake."

When the two of them arrived at the Imam's headquarters the following day, they felt extremely uneasy. There were no women around, only men who looked stressed while going about their business. Everyone they spoke to looked at them with suspicion. They were made to wait in a sitting area for more than an hour before they could see someone in an official capacity they could talk to.

They were finally led to an office where a bearded man in his forties was sitting behind his desk.

"You asked to speak to someone from the Movement. How can I help you?" he said with a stern face.

Sana told him that she was Ramzi's fiancée and that she was worried about him and wanted to know if there were any new developments regarding the disappearance of the Imam and his entourage. The man asked Sana a few questions to ascertain she actually knew Ramzi and then said in a serious tone:

"We don't divulge information about the Imam or his entourage to anyone, and I mean anyone!"

"But sir, please take pity and tell me what you know about Ramzi's whereabouts," Sana said and tears came falling down her cheeks.

"Are you deaf? I told you I am in no position to give information about anything to you, especially to do with official security matters of the Imam," the man said angrily.

He paused for a moment and said curtly, "I can't help you. Please leave."

But as Sana and Fatima turned around to leave, he seemed to have felt sorry for her when he added: "Sister, I advise you to get on with your life. Allah is Great!"

Fatima helped Sana get out of the building. She was staggering and needed support. Fatima quickly flagged a taxi and tried to comfort her.

"Don't lose hope, Sana. As long as their bodies have not surfaced, Ramzi can still be alive."

"You don't understand. I know it in my heart. And the man we just spoke to knows – he confirmed it for me. Ramzi's gone and I don't know what to do about it."

That night in bed Sana cried so much that by dawn her tears had dried up. Should she be getting dressed to go to the university? What use was her nursing degree now? Ramzi had given up his studies for her sake – that's how he was. She was at the end of finishing her degree. Ramzi would have wanted her to finish her degree even if she didn't have the willingness anymore. She was in a perfect happy dream when she was with Ramzi. Now, she had woken up to the reality she was in – her heart shattered into a thousand pieces. Still, she couldn't give up on him. She needed to find that lit candle flickering in the far corners of her mind.

CHAPTER 19
SANA AND RAMZI

Winter 2015

S ana put a bit of cream on her sagging cheeks and wore
her black scarf. She had stopped wearing make-up ever
since she performed the Hajj pilgrimage in Mecca and
opted to cover her head. It was prescribed by her religion,
wasn't it? It didn't come to her naturally but living in Abu
Dhabi for so many years, where a lot of Arab women wore
the headscarf and almost all Emirati women did, it seemed
a lot easier for her. Did it really matter what she looked like?
After four pregnancies, her small body frame had accumu-
lated so much fat that it was difficult to get back to her
old shape. She looked at her face once more in the mirror.
She categorized herself as an old woman now, much nearer
death, but she had died already when Ramzi disappeared
without a trace, years and years ago.

She had stalled her parents for two years after Ramzi's
disappearance, with the faint hope that he would re-appear
one day. Her parents had hounded her on a daily basis

to marry Ahmad, her father's cousin's son, reminding her that she had already graduated from nursing school and that she would soon be past the right marrying age. For two years she came up with a number of excuses, mainly to do with training requirements at the hospital where she worked. She got away with it partly because Ahmad had found a job in Abu Dhabi and would only come to visit his family twice a year. On his last visit to Beirut, it was agreed by the two families that Sana and Ahmad would get married during his following visit. On that day, she didn't know whether it was just a coincidence or her unconsciously clinging to the hope of seeing Ramzi again, but she was wearing the same black dress with the big red flower brooch she wore on her last date with Ramzi. As soon as Ahmad and his family left, she went to her room and immediately ripped the brooch and threw it on the floor. A large hole appeared where the brooch had been. She undressed and tore the ruined dress to pieces out of utter frustration and helplessness. She fetched a plastic carrier bag, put the torn pieces in it and got rid of it immediately so her mother couldn't see it. The following day, Sana could no longer dodge the issue of her marriage to Ahmad and accepted the proposal when asked outright by her father. She acquiesced because she no longer cared about what happened to her. As her wedding day neared, she did think of taking her own life, but was ashamed of herself for even having considered doing such an act. She knew she was not strong enough to go through with it anyway. And she knew weaklings like her did not have the strength to impose their will on others but were steered by the people around them.

Her wedding was a grand affair. She had a large, extended family and everyone was invited to the big do at a famous hotel in Beirut after the marriage agreement was signed. Ahmad had proposed to her face-to-face a few days before the wedding – just a formality she had to go through. As was the Muslim custom, Ahmad suggested a large sum of money in case he divorced her. Her father intervened and said it was not necessary and that he was already part of the family. As a token sum, 100 Lebanese Liras was adequate, her father said and her fate was thus sealed. Ahmad gave her a large diamond ring on the occasion. He showered her with lots of other presents from Abu Dhabi. Her parents also bought her new clothing and everything a new bride needed save for household stuff because she was going to live in Abu Dhabi with Ahmad.

The hardest part for Sana was the honeymoon in Cyprus. Ahmad had booked a suite at the Hilton Hotel in Nicosia for that purpose. Being intimate with Ahmad was the last thing she wanted to do, but she had to go through with it. Fortunately, Ahmad, who was 4 years her senior, treaded with caution and treated her with such kindness and affection that she felt guilty. On the first night they spent together, Ahmad put down her awkwardness to shyness and inexperience. Sana, though, began a process that she adopted for all the following years to come. She compartmentalized her mind. She locked Ramzi in one corner of her brain – a place only she was allowed to go. When she was with Ahmad, she would lock that door on Ramzi and forget that it was there. She had to.

And over the years, she came to the realization that sexual urges were like eating and sleeping. Love was a feeling apart – no matter what form it took. And passion – the one she had for Ramzi. That sort of passion shared between two people was a rarity. It was love and beyond that few people experienced, she was certain. It was the stuff that was described in books and could not be replicated in life easily. She thanked Allah for giving her Ramzi even for a short while. And every time she prayed and asked Allah to safeguard her family, she would also pray for Ramzi's soul. She had concluded a long time ago that he was dead. If he weren't, he would have found her by now. He would never have given up on her. What tormented her most was the unknown. Not knowing how he actually died. She had imagined all sorts of nightmares, but it only made her ill. And she still carried the guilt of a culprit in her heart.

It took her a good year to adjust to life in Abu Dhabi. 'I don't want you to work. I earn enough for the both of us. We need to start a family', Ahmad had told her the minute they arrived in Abu Dhabi. She agreed with him knowing fully-well that juggling the duties of a nurse with those of rearing children was a near impossibility. In those early days, Ahmad was jealous, too. The first time she'd mentioned going to work to him, he had dismissed it by saying he didn't like her working with male doctors and nurses. By the end of the first year in Abu Dhabi, she was pregnant. She bore children like clockwork – every two years. The first two were boys, the next two girls. She had discovered the joys of motherhood and that's what kept her going and filled her days. She could never envisage how fulfilled she felt. The first ten years of marriage were so busy for her that she didn't even have time to think about anything else but looking after her brood. She spent the next twenty years, and all her energy, on guiding her children – making sure they did well at school, that they were properly cared for and that they became well-rounded adults. She had succeeded in her mission. Her sons, in their 30's, both civil engineers, had secured jobs in reputable companies in Abu Dhabi after returning from their studies in the USA. They had each found a partner amongst the growing number of Lebanese living in the Emirates and were already fathers. Her elder daughter, a pharmacist, had just got married and her youngest, a business analyst, was happily married and had given birth to her youngest grandchild.

Nearing retirement age, it was Ahmad who had suggested the Hajj pilgrimage. 'Let's do it. We're so near Saudi Arabia and it's the easiest travelling we can do these days. We don't know what's going to happen to us in the future – we may not be in good health and may be unable to undertake the journey. It's one of the five pillars of Islam', he'd told her. Sana was of the same opinion. She wanted to go on the Hajj pilgrimage. She wanted to thank Allah for bestowing upon her the joy of having children even if He'd taken Ramzi from her. Her lost love was replaced by her unconditional love for each and every one of her children and grandchildren.

When Nora called her and said she would be working in Dubai for three months, Sana nearly fell off her chair out of sheer surprise. She promised Nora she'd arrange to see her and would travel to Dubai from Abu Dhabi. But Sana didn't drive. She asked her younger daughter to drive her to Dubai for the meeting with Nora. Nora was the only one of her old friends she was still in touch with but not on a regular basis. Nora sent her a card or a short note every few years and never mentioned Ramzi and rarely mentioned the others. Sana wrote to Nora every time she had a new-born and then sent her a letter once a year to tell her how her children were growing up. Upon learning that Nora would be spending some time in Dubai, she was so overjoyed that she couldn't sleep a wink that first night in anticipation of seeing her again. They agreed to meet at a well-known café in one of the big shopping malls of Dubai.

When Sana arrived at the café on the set date, Nora was already there. Sana had no trouble in recognizing her although they hadn't seen each other for so many years. Nora hadn't changed much. Sana immediately leaned forward and gave her a hug. Overwhelmed by their emotions, both of them couldn't hold back their tears and then each stepped back and gave each other tearful smiles.

"Oh…this is my younger daughter, Huda, and my one-year-old grandson," Sana said, wiping her tears.

"I'm Nora. Very pleased to meet you Huda and your lovely boy," Nora said and extended her hand.

"The pleasure is mine. I've heard a lot about you from Mum," Huda said. "I'll let you get on with it. You've got lots to talk about. Mum, give me a call when you're ready to go. I'll be at the children's play area," she said and took her leave, steering the pushchair.

As soon as they sat down and ordered their coffees, Sana said something that Nora didn't expect to hear.

"Don't judge me too harshly, Nora. I chose to wear the headscarf three years ago when I performed the Hajj pilgrimage with Ahmad."

"I'm not here to judge you harshly or otherwise," said Nora. "Please don't think that way. Who am I to judge you?

I'm here to see you and I don't care how you look like or what you're wearing."

"You haven't changed a bit. You're still the girl who was so sure of herself – the one I admired and looked up to. I wish I had the confidence you had and still have. My life would have been completely different."

"Come now, Sana, you're the one who's being harsh on yourself!"

"Am I? Ramzi was the dreamer. I was the one who had her feet firmly on the ground – the practical one. Some people might say that's a good personality trait. I wouldn't have survived the loss of Ramzi if I didn't have it, I guess."

"You're the one to be admired, Sana. You were able to create a new life for yourself and a loving family."

"I don't think I'm that great, Nora. I married a man despite not being in love with him. I studied nursing and barely practiced it because I became a housewife. I had four children and let myself go. I'm now a fat grandmother who has kept the most important thing that happened in her life a secret from her parents, her husband, and her children."

"But you do love your children and grandchildren, don't you? My life would be completely empty without my daughter," Nora said.

"Of course, I do! I love them to bits and I have absolute affection towards my husband. He has always treated me like his princess. May Allah give him health and a long life! What I'm saying is I feel like I'm living someone else's life. My life should have been lived with Ramzi…"

"It was not your fault Ramzi disappeared," Nora said and was glad to have used the word 'disappeared' instead of 'is dead'. It had been years that everyone knew the Imam and his entourage were killed or got rid of somehow. Their bodies were never found and the details of their killings were never truly discovered even after regime change in Libya and the murder of Kaddafi.

"It was entirely my fault that he died, Nora. It was for me that he became the bodyguard of the Imam. It was for me that he gave up studying nursing. It was his ardent yearning for us to be together that he sacrificed himself for," Sana said and her tears began flowing again.

"Don't do this to yourself, Sana."

"I'm sorry to break down like this. This is the first time I've cried for Ramzi in years. I cannot forget him until my last breath – you do understand, don't you? I haven't talked about him to anyone but you since I got married. Sometimes when I think of him, I feel I'm just going to explode – like a bomb ticking inside me. It's terrible. It's like a recurring nightmare."

"But you have survived even with all the pain."

"I have survived because I'm living through my children and now my grandchildren as well," Sana said and wiped her tears.

"It's probably the same for me – my only happiness in life has been my daughter and I can look forward to holding a grandchild soon, I hope. My daughter is living with a very kind man and they plan to get married next year."

"I'm glad to hear. May Allah protect them!"

"Sana, I'm a lot like you. I haven't been lucky in love in this life either. You at least have a caring husband. My relationships never worked. You know how Tony left me for Carole…"

"I'm so sad for you, my dear friend. The death of Waleed had something to do with it, I'm sure."

"Perhaps – I don't know. All I know is we can't turn the clock back and do things differently or change fate. It's no use saying 'if the civil war didn't take place in Lebanon, our lives would have taken a completely different course'."

"So very true – one can only say that it's Allah's Will. I realized that in Mecca. I can't rebel against what is 'written' for me. I wish I can say I will meet Ramzi again in my next life, but my religion doesn't believe in reincarnation. All I can hope for is that I will meet him again on Judgment Day and that Allah will forgive my sins in this life."

CHAPTER 20
CITÉ UNIVERSITAIRE

Academic Year 1976-77

For a student, the best place to stay in Paris is the Cité Universitaire, the collective student residence campus. Not only does it have the best campus in Paris with its beautiful grounds, but it also has four university restaurants. On its vast grounds are the so called 'houses' of some 30 countries, like the American House and the Franco-British House. Each country 'house' accommodates their own nationals but with a quota that allows students from other countries to stay there as well. It is located at the edge of Paris, in the 14th Arrondissement, close to the Porte d'Orléans metro station, making it easily accessible from anywhere in Paris. Waleed, Carole, Tony, and Nora had waited patiently to get entry when they applied for accommodation at the beginning of September of that year once they received their university acceptance letters. All four had already visited some of the 'houses' where students they knew had been previously admitted. They loved the atmosphere and cama-raderie that they witnessed and wanted to be part of it.

Carole, Waleed, and Tony got their approvals to be housed at the Lebanese House a few weeks after they applied. Nora wished to live at the Lebanese House, too, so she could be with her close friends, but had to choose the Armenian House instead. She had applied for a grant from an Armenian benevolent association to cover the cost of her rent, but the association would only pay if she were housed at the Armenian House. Nora's approval came at the very last minute because of the formalities tied to obtaining the grant. She loved the Armenian House the minute she saw it. In the vicinity of the Netherlands House and the Cambodian House, it was one of the first built in the Cité in the 1930's. It had one of the best architectural designs on campus, mod-elled on the architecture of Armenian churches. The Leba-nese House, with its 60's architecture, was at the far end of the Cité Universitaire, quite a way from the Armenian House. Tony had assured Nora that it didn't matter. 'I'll come and see you whenever my schedule permits', he'd told her.

The day before they left the Alésia studio, all four were busy sorting and packing their gear for the move to the Cité which took them practically the whole day. Tony and Nora knew it was their last night in the same bed. Soon after din-ner, they didn't want to waste any time and climbed up to the suspended bed. Unable to fall asleep, they lay there silently holding each other tightly. Carole and Waleed, sleeping on the floor below them were silent, too, for a while until the studio's usual night-time silence was broken by the sounds of kissing and then heavy panting coming from Waleed. This was followed by Waleed making gnarling sounds like a wild animal mating. And when he came, he let out a cry that Nora was certain was that of a creature from the depths of a wild forest. Tony and Nora had not heard a single sound coming out of Carole, but the noises Waleed made were amplified in Nora's ears and sounded like an army of men howling.

"What's the matter with Waleed? He's never done this before." Nora whispered into Tony's ear, unable to hide her shock and embarrassment.

"Shhhhhh," Tony silenced her. "Sleep!" he ordered her and kissed her gently on the lips before she could protest.

They were all up very early in the morning.

"We'll go and get some croissants," Waleed said, oblivious of his behaviour during the night. Both Tony and Nora registered the embarrassment on Carole's face. She then squinted as if to say she was sorry for what had happened. Waleed didn't notice the expression on her face. He dragged her to the door, and they were gone.

"What's wrong with Waleed again? I thought he had got over his depression whilst living in this studio."

"Don't make a big thing out of it, Nora. You know he's prone to getting depressed. He must have felt frustrated. He liked the four of us living here in the studio. I guess it's harder for him to accept that he won't be living so freely with Carole at the Cité."

"I fear he's emotionally too fragile and his behaviour of last night is not normal. I told you before to convince him to get psychiatric treatment for whatever he's suffering from. They have excellent doctors here and it's free. I'm sure it's caused by something that happened to him in childhood," Nora mused.

"Just drop it!" Tony yelled.

"Why are you so agitated when we talk about Waleed? This is the second time you've yelled at me. What is wrong with you? You're a rational person and it's so unlike you not to see that I'm talking sense here. Why do you get upset whenever I bring up Waleed's depressive state?"

Tony had trouble explaining to Nora why he got all worked up about the issue. He immediately realised that his losing his temper was unacceptable. After apologising profusely, he calmly added:

"Please, Nora, can you just forget what happened last night? We're all human and make mistakes or behave badly. He'll be okay once we settle at the Cité."

The next three weeks were happy times. All four spent their days together doing things that they enjoyed. It seemed like summer holidays before classes started at the university. Waleed was elated that he was able to secure a room all for himself at the Lebanese House. He could have Carole there any time he wanted and his privacy. Although these rooms were usually given to graduate students, he was able to get one on the strength of the director of the house being a childhood friend of his father's. And his parents could afford to pay the higher rent. Carole shared a room with another Lebanese female student but spent most of her time in Waleed's room. Tony was assigned a room which he shared with a male African student with whom he eventually became good friends. Although not housed in the same place, Nora didn't mind this as long as she could spend most of her days with her three friends.

The carefree days came to an abrupt end with the start of classes. It was no longer possible to spend all day and every day together. To everyone's dismay, all four had been admitted to different universities in Paris and had different schedules. Added to this, both Tony and Nora had to find part-time work to cover their daily expenses. Waleed forbade Carole from doing any part-time work even though she needed to. He said his parents sent him enough money to cover the costs of both him and Carole. After doing odd jobs, like counting cars on a highway at night, Tony found a waiter's regular part-time job at a Greek restaurant in the vicinity of Rue du Mouffetard, famed for its numerous eateries. He'd do the evening meal shift from 6 pm to 11 pm every night, sometimes until midnight on Saturdays, except for Mondays when the restaurant was closed.

Babysitters were very much in demand with urban families in Greater Paris and Nora found a babysitting job in a matter of a few days. It was very well paid – by the hour, with food thrown in. It was in one of the chic suburbs of Paris and involved looking after not one but two 18-month-old twin girls. The mother of the twins, a skinny lady, had poor health and a badly curved spine because of carrying two babies for nine months. And although she had quit her job, looking after two babies in the early months had also taken its toll on her. She needed respite every afternoon and time for the treatment of her back. Luckily, Nora had her classes scheduled in the morning. But commuting back and forth to a Parisian suburb was hard. It meant she had to put in at least 2 hours travelling time every day. This was every day except for Sundays.

Looking after twins was not easy either, but she did her best. Upon arrival, she would take them for a stroll at a nearby park in their linked pushchairs. When they returned, she would give them a bath. That was difficult to juggle. She had to make sure the babies didn't catch cold. She seated and secured one of the babies in the high chair. She bathed the other and quickly dressed her. She ran some more hot water in the bathtub to make sure it hadn't gone cold and then bathed and dressed the second baby. She then gave them their dinner, which was fortunately prepared by their mother earlier in the day. All Nora had to do was heat it up. Once they ate their meal, she would put them to bed and wait until their mother's return. After months of doing this, the whole process was no longer a chore. She didn't mind the work especially since she had got attached to the cute little ones. Years later, Nora would remember them and wonder how she could manage to look after the twins when she had a hard time looking after her own daughter. 'When one is young, one is fearless', she'd murmured to herself.

It was no longer possible to see her friends every day and Nora missed Tony terribly. By the time she came back to the Cité at around 8 pm, he would be at the restaurant. She was too tired to walk all the way to the Lebanese House to see Carole and Waleed. Hence, the only time she could get together with Tony was Sunday during the day, which meant lunchtime because Tony inevitably didn't come back from work before 1 am and needed his sleep. Now and again, Carole, Waleed, and Nora visited Tony at the restaurant on a Saturday night. They'd go as patrons and eat dinner there. The owner of the Greek restaurant normally charged them a nominal price – 'student price' he'd say with a smile. Not only was he thoroughly satisfied with Tony's work in the restaurant but also with Waleed because he brought his guitar along and sang a few songs. The owner of the restaurant was pleased that his customers were entertained on a Saturday night and proudly introduced Waleed by saying 'Our Saturday night live act!'

Months passed with their usual daily routine in place. When spring came, it did not bring with it the happiness associated with the season. And things started to unravel. Up until then, Nora had gladly plodded along with her studies and the babysitting job. She looked forward to the short meetings with Tony. Sometimes Tony would take her to the cinema on a Monday, before his evening shift, for an early showing and then a quick bite to eat if it was official holidays and she didn't have to babysit. Other times, she'd sneak him into her room at the Armenian House when her roommate was not around. Tony would kiss her tenderly and caress her hair and say, 'I missed you my sweet girl'.

One Sunday morning, Tony turned up at her door unexpectedly.

"What are you doing here at this time? Weren't we supposed to meet for lunch?"

"Change of plan. I got up early and thought we can have a picnic on campus! It's glorious Spring weather!" Tony announced, enthusiastically, with a big grin on his face.

He showed her the bag of food he had bought and asked if she had a spare blanket they could use as a spread. They headed out to the area he had previously spotted – a large green grass expanse at the edge of the campus. Tony said he'd asked Carole and Waleed to come as well and that they'd be there soon. Eventually, it was only Carole who turned up.

"Where's Waleed?"

"He didn't want to come. He got so angry when I insisted that he raised his hand and I thought he was going to slap me like he did in Beirut. He's in one of those depressive moods again," Carole said and sighed.

"We need to persuade him to see a psychiatrist," Nora said boldly.

"As if he'd listen to me or to any of us – he's so stubborn. These bouts of depression are getting more frequent and I really don't know what to do anymore," Carole said and looked at both of them as if waiting for a solution to the problem.

"He'll be okay soon. Forgive him, Carole. He always surmounts his depression – you know that. Let's not spoil our picnic – brunch is served!" Tony said and gave Nora a look that meant she should not pursue the issue any longer.

Carole stayed for a good two hours. She ate and drank with them, chatted about her studies and how things were going at her university, but they could tell her mind was somewhere else. Once the meal was finished, she excused herself.

"I need to go back. I really shouldn't leave Waleed on his own for more than a couple of hours," she said and left.

"Don't start again!" Tony said knowing very well that Nora wanted to discuss Waleed's situation with him. He poured her another glass of wine. With a defeated look on her face, Nora bent over and gave him a kiss on the cheek.

"You know my sister's married to a Canadian national and was granted Canadian citizenship. She recently vouched for me to facilitate things with my immigration application. The Canadian Embassy contacted me a few weeks ago and I went for an interview last Monday."

"You didn't tell me," Nora said accusatively.

"Well, I didn't want to tell you before the interview."

"So, what happened?"

"I passed the interview! I'm in! It's only a matter of waiting for a few months for the paperwork. I will finally be immigrating to Canada!"

He seemed so excited and happy. So, this was the reason for organizing the picnic – to celebrate the good news.

"Congratulations!" Nora said with enthusiasm, trying to hide her displeasure.

"I need to put aside as much money as I can before I leave for Canada. Maybe I need to do the lunch shift at the restaurant as well. I'm going to stop going to the university. It's of no use to me now. The courses I've taken here won't be counted in Canada anyway. It's not the usual North American course credit system here in France."

Nora felt happy for him but sad in her heart at the same time. She knew about his desire to immigrate to Canada, but the news of his imminent departure struck her hard – as if a ton of bricks had fallen on her head. Will she lose him after all? She drummed up the courage to say something about herself.

"How am I going to live without you here if you leave for Canada?"

"Nora, let's cross the hurdles one at a time. Once I get my papers, I need to go to Canada and figure things out first and familiarize myself with their educational system. It won't be difficult to continue your studies there if you want to. But it might take some time for me to arrange all that. We may have to be apart for at least a year. Can you be patient? Would you consider joining me in Canada?"

"I would love to," she said, thrilled that his future plans included her. "I don't mind the wait as long as we will be together in the end."

"Don't worry too much, Nora. We'll work things out," is the last thing he said on the subject.

CHAPTER 21

THE DAMNED

The following months, until the summer break, Waleed didn't show up to any of the outings Nora and Tony had planned. Carole turned up alone every time. She would have an excuse for Waleed not turning up. She'd say something like 'he's got the flu' or 'he's preparing for an exam' or give some other lame excuse. When Nora challenged her one day, it was Tony who responded: "Don't make a fuss again, Nora. I see him every day and he's fine. He just likes to stay in his room and loves to entertain himself by playing the guitar. Why don't you go and see him yourself one of these days? You're so busy with your studies and babysitting that you can't be bothered to visit him. Why blame Carole?" Nora was upset with Tony's response but didn't show it. She never brought up the subject of Waleed after that.

Nora's babysitting job ended just before the university final exam results were out. The mother of the twins told her their old nanny was coming back to work for her after a year off due to illness. The Beirut International Airport had reopened and Nora's family insisted she come home for the summer holidays. Nora decided to go and see her friends at the Lebanese House the Sunday before she left for Beirut. When she got there, she found all three in Waleed's room.

"Tell us about your results," Tony said after greeting her with a warm hug.

"I passed!" Nora said and then giggled.

"I don't have to worry about that now. I'm no longer a university student until I get to Canada that is," Tony said and gave her another hug.

"I passed too, but Waleed has failed all his courses. He's been cutting classes and that's the result. He'll have to repeat the year if he's allowed," Carole said in a sad tone.

"I'm sure he'll be allowed. Don't be too tough on him, Carole, he'll pull through," Tony said.

Nora looked at Waleed. She hadn't seen him in months and he looked like death-warmed-up. He looked so pale and haggard that she was astounded.

"You've lost so much weight!"

"He's skin and bone," Carole butted in. "He eats like a sparrow."

"You'll be a good candidate for the skinniest person in the world in the Guinness Book of Records," Nora joked.

"Stop pulling his leg. He's as handsome as ever," said Tony.

There was no response from Waleed. They were talking about him and he sat there with a dead-pan face, not responding to anything that was said about him. Nora took a few steps forward and faced him directly.

"Did you miss me at all?" Nora tilted her head and looked him straight in the eye.

She could finally prize a reaction from Waleed. He walked slowly towards her with a half-smile and gave her a friendly hug. But Nora felt there was something inherently sad in his comportment. She couldn't put her finger on it. Waleed and Carole told her next they were not going to Beirut for the summer holidays. Waleed said they were planning to travel to Belgium and Holland and then sarcastically added, "I'll never set foot in Lebanon again."

"How about you, Tony?" Nora knew the answer but she wished he'd come with her.

"You know I can't go. I'll be working full-time at the restaurant."

After she said goodbye to Waleed and Carole, Tony walked her back to the Armenian House.

"The situation is calm now in Beirut, but fighting can erupt at any time because nothing is settled. Come back as soon as you can," he said.

"You'll still be here, won't you?"

"Of course, I will. It will take months before my Canadian papers arrive. So, don't think much about anything. Enjoy seeing your parents."

"I'll miss you. I really don't want to go but I have to."

Tony hugged her one last time. He then held her hand gently and kissed her on the lips tenderly.

"I hope you have a safe journey. I'll be waiting for your return."

⊰⊱

Nora spent two months in Beirut that Summer. She was happy to reunite with her parents and brother. She realized how much she'd missed them. She went to the beach and shopping with her mother. She saw a couple of her old schoolmates – the normal things that she did before the civil war began. She also visited Tony's parents and gave them the present that he had sent them. But she was always in fear that fighting might re-start. She'd be stuck in Beirut and not be able to go back to Paris. Save for a car bomb in her area that unfortunately claimed the lives of scores of people, there were no major incidents. And although she'd enjoyed seeing her parents, when the time came, she was happy to be leaving Lebanon again.

When she landed at Orly Airport in Paris on a Monday, both Tony and Carole were waiting for her. Nora was so happy to see them that she burst into tears.

"I thought I might not be able to make it back," she told them.

On their way to the Cité Universitaire, Nora described to them how things were back in Beirut and then asked about what they were both up to. Tony said he was glad to be working full-time at the Greek restaurant and that he was able to finally save some money.

"Where's Waleed? Why didn't he come with you? Did you go to Belgium and Holland?"

"We did go to Belgium and Holland, but upon our return Waleed got really sick. He was so weak that he developed bronchitis after a simple flu," Carole said with teary eyes.

"It was really bad and he had to be hospitalised. He was released from hospital only two days ago," said Tony.

"I'm really sorry to hear this. But when I saw him last before I went to Beirut, he didn't look good. He looked so emaciated."

"Let's get something nice to eat to celebrate your return," Tony said, clearly signalling to Nora to change the subject. The next couple of weeks, before the start of her second academic year at the university, Nora spent time looking for another babysitting job. She found one when she'd almost given up because most offers were for locations too far from Paris. The job was exactly what she was looking for. The location was ideal too – in the 15th Arrondissement, not far from where she lived. It involved looking after a boy of four and a half years old. The job entailed similar duties to the one she had when she was looking after the twins except for picking him up from kindergarten every afternoon at 4 pm during the week. The boy's father, a banker, looked after him on Saturdays. Both parents were off on Sundays and his mother, a hairdresser, would look after him on Mondays, her day off instead of Saturdays. This was the best thing about the job. It meant that Nora had Mondays free, the same as Tony, and they'd be able to spend more time together.

And they did. Nora was so content that she pushed aside all her anxiety about Tony leaving for Canada. They'd go to the movies and a meal afterwards or walk in the Luxembourg Gardens or the Père Lachaise Cemetery. They made sure they didn't miss important exhibitions at the Louvre or any other museum that was open on Mondays. Sometimes Carole would join them but never Waleed. Nora saw Waleed only if they had bought takeaway food and took it back to the Lebanese House. They ate their meal in Waleed's room. Although he'd recovered fully from bronchitis, he still looked undernourished. He was gaunt and his face always looked pale. She'd observe him when they ate. He'd take a couple of mouthfuls and then stop.

"You need to eat more. You need to get out of this room, Waleed. You need to get some colour on your face," Nora told him once. He didn't answer her. He just smiled, and fetching his guitar, he sang a song that he knew she particularly liked.

It was a gloomy Monday, one of those overcast and sad days in Paris. Tony and Nora had not met the previous Monday. Strangely, Tony had called her to say he was feeling too tired and wanted to catch up on his sleep. 'Let's see each other next Monday', he'd said. They had agreed to visit a bookshop that sold old and antique books – just out of curiosity. Tony had said he'd pick her up at 10 am. It was 11 am and he hadn't turned up. By 11:30, she was too restless to wait any longer. She thought he might be really sick. It was so unlike him not to turn up like this. So she walked to the Lebanese House. When she climbed the stairs to the floor where Tony, Carole and Waleed had their rooms, there was mayhem. The large corridor was full of students, whispering and gesticulating. She spotted a couple of tall gendarmes in full gear guarding Waleed's door. Alarmed, she turned left and headed towards Tony's room in a hurry. Just at that moment, Tony's door opened and out came two men in dark suits – they looked like policemen in civilian clothing. She went in and there was Tony, sitting on his bed. He looked up. His eyes were red as if he'd spent the whole night drinking. He stood up and walked towards her. He held both her hands.

"Waleed is dead. He committed suicide," he said in tears.

"Why did he do such a silly thing?" is all she could say. She felt her knees would give away and she'd fall. She felt like throwing up.

"It was me who found his lifeless body this morning, Nora..."

She hugged him tightly and they both sobbed.

"Excuse me. We have to go now." It was one of the policemen in civilian clothing at the door.

"Nora, I have to go to the police station. They need my statement. They may ask you to come in too, later. I think they will interview all his friends. Don't panic. Just tell them the truth. Carole is being looked after by a couple of female students. Find her!"

Nora looked for Carole everywhere. She knocked on all the student rooms, but she was not in any of them. She went to the administrator and asked about Carole. He said she was in his anteroom. He'd called in a doctor who had given her sedatives. He told her she was asleep and directed Nora to the anteroom and left. Nora went and sat next to the tiny bed where Carole lay. She looked peaceful in her sleep. Even though Carole could not feel it, Nora held her hand as she felt the urge of consoling her. How could another tragedy befall them? It seemed to her that no matter where they were, the cursed destiny was following them all the way from Lebanon. Nora sat there for hours without moving and there was no end to her tears.

━━✛━━

The previous night

"Look at what you've done now! You're despicable! I'd beat you up to a pulp if I weren't your friend, Waleed."

Tony's words kept on coming back in Waleed's head like a scratched disc being played over and over again. What the hell was so wrong with him? Why did he always have to make terrible mistakes? Why was he so stupid? Why was he so selfish? Waleed walked up and down the length of his room. His knees soon bothered him. There was no strength in them. They couldn't carry the weight of his skinny body. He sat down on his bed and taking out a cigarette paper, he placed some tobacco on it and added the bit of dope that was the last of the batch he had bought in Amsterdam. He rolled the paper and lit the cigarette. He took a couple of drags. He got up and looked for the bottle of vodka. When he finally found it, he sat down on his bed again and took a big gulp out of the bottle. He'll soon feel fine. He must.

He stood up again and fetched his guitar. He sat on his bed again. He drank some more vodka and started to play. His guitar, his lifelong companion – this would make him feel better. The first image of Carole – running, her flame hair in a pony tail, swaying – that's the image he never wanted to forget. He felt a sharp pain in his chest. How could he get rid of the pain? The dope cigarette was no longer lit. He lit it again and took a couple more drags. This should do it. He resumed playing the guitar. He played one song after another until his fragile fingers couldn't move anymore. He laid his guitar on the bed. He drank some more vodka and sucked on his cigarette.

He closed his eyes and saw himself as a little boy. His mother was holding his hand and saying what a good boy he was. Suddenly a dark man appeared and snatched her. She disappeared in a puff. He saw pinks and reds – all shades. It was the colour of his mother's lipstick, and Carole's hair, yes, yes, but also, disturbingly, like in a movie, he saw Michel's final moment – the colour of the blood that came out of his body when he was shot...and that other man's blood...

He opened his eyes. Why wasn't he feeling any better? This dope is rubbish – fake dope – not like the hasheesh from Lebanon. That must be it. Waleed reached for the vodka bottle again and drank some more. He neither believed in the Druze faith nor in that of the Christians. Hell, he didn't even believe in the existence of God! Why did he carry the feeling of guilt? He now realized guilt had a stronger hold on him than love. How could he get rid of it now? Was he cursed by the gods? Was fate playing tricks on him? Ah...nonsense – he didn't believe in such a primitive thing called fate. You made your fate and you suffered the consequences of your actions.

He took one last drag. No more dope. He had drunk three quarters of the vodka bottle and felt like peeing. He went to the bathroom. While urinating, his eye caught the shaving blade on the side of the washbasin. It was one of those expensive ones with a tortoise shell cover that his father had bought for him from a fancy shop in Paris when he started shaving regularly. He still used it after all these years although he didn't shave that often now – once every two weeks. The blade was very sharp and as good as it was when brand new. When he finished with the bathroom, he took the blade with him to bed. He lay there, next to his guitar.

His mind got muddled again. He kept seeing all these reds when he closed his eyes. He sat up and drank the last bit of vodka in two gulps. He slowly stretched himself on his bed and thought of Carole. All that mattered to him in this life was her and nothing else. And yet, he had given her a hard time for months. Not only that but he had made the biggest of all blunders. He was willing to carry all the guilt, no matter what, in this life if she could forgive him. But he knew what he'd done could not be forgiven, especially by her.

Even if she forgave him, what kind of life would he be able to give her? All he had to offer her was a life of guilt. He didn't deserve her or her devotion even if she forgave him. He closed his eyes and the reds returned. It's too painful to continue like this – he must spare Carole from partaking in the pain.

He swivelled the tortoise shell protective cover. The sharp blade was so shiny that he could see himself in it. It was like looking at his face in a mirror. He used all his strength and cut the vein of his left wrist open. It wasn't as painful as he'd thought it would be after all. But he didn't look. He took a deep breath and did the same to his right wrist. His head slowly fell back on his pillow and his right arm on his guitar. The red blood gushed out and trickled into the sound hole of his guitar.

CHAPTER 22
CAROLE

When Tony and Nora got to Hamilton, it was already afternoon. Tony said visiting hours at the hospital would soon be over and suggested postponing the visit to the following day.

"You're too tired. Why don't I take you to the hotel and I'll go to the hospital? It's best to check in and have a nap perhaps. I'll pick you up later and we can have dinner together."

"I'm feeling alright now. My headache's gone. I want to go to the hospital straightaway, Tony."

"Are you sure?"

"Yes. I can't wait to see Carole."

But the minute she stepped out of the car in front of the hospital, Nora felt she was having an anxiety attack. She was apprehensive. She walked slowly until they reached the ward where Carole's room was. And what she saw shook her so intensely that for a moment she thought she was hallucinating. There he was, leaning against the wall next to Carole's room door. Waleed had come back to life. It was Paul

– the same height, the same lean figure, the same curly hair even though Paul wore it shorter. She leaned slightly forward to take a good look at his face – unbelievable! How could someone be so identical to one's father? 'I've got to control my emotions', Nora said to herself.

"This is Paul, my son, and this is Nora," Tony introduced them with an earnest expression on his face.

"Pleased to meet you," Paul said.

"Uh…me too," Nora said and shook his hand, not daring to look at his face for too long.

"I've got to go, Dad. I'll be here tomorrow morning," he said and without waiting for the response, he turned around and left, with a hand held high up as a sign of saying goodbye.

That gesture, that nonchalant behaviour, was Waleed to a tee. Not only did Paul resemble his father, he also behaved like him. 'This can't be!' Nora murmured to herself.

"What did you say?"

"Nothing – you go in first, Tony. Tell Carole I'm here. Give me a few minutes and I'll follow you."

What was waiting for her behind that door? No matter how old she was, she could never be completely ready for something like this. Nora took a deep breath and opened the door. She went in, took a few steps and stood still for a moment and looked at her shoes. She had always felt uncomfortable in hospitals. They were, other than maternity wards, unhappy places even if they were spotlessly clean and had the best equipment. She heard the sound of sheets and she looked up and met Tony's eyes. He gestured for her to come forward.

"Nora!" She then heard Carole's frail voice calling her. She had one of her hands stretched out.

She now hastily approached Carole's bed. Tony was standing on the other side of the bed. She took the stretched-out hand, unable to say anything. Carole extended her other hand to hug her. She leaned forward and let Carole hold her. Neither could control the flow of their tears.

"I'll let the two of you talk. I'll be near the coffee machine at the end of the corridor if you need me," Tony said after a while and left.

Carole let go of her and gestured that she should sit on the chair next to her bed. Nora obeyed her.

"I'm so happy that you came all the way from Paris to see me," Carole said, still crying.

"I'm happy to see you after all these years," Nora said and noticing a tissue box on the table next to her, she pulled some tissues out and gave them to Carole.

"I've changed a lot, haven't I?" Carole said.

Nora looked at Carole's face. Yes, she had changed a great deal. She had lost so much weight that she was unrecognizable. She hadn't lost her hair with the cancer treatment as yet. She had it cut very short and her once healthy red hair had thinned and lost its lustre. Her face had literally lost all its muscles. She was so gaunt that her wrinkles and freckles seemed more pronounced. Her once beautiful green eyes had sunk into deep sockets. Nora stretched her hand and held Carole's hand tenderly. The freckles on her hand and arm had grown much larger than she remembered from the old days.

"I look old, don't I?"

"Don't say things like that. You're ill – that's all. You'll get better."

"I won't get better. I know it. When I was diagnosed with cancer, they said I was in its last stage. So, there's no hope for me even if they're trying with this experimental treatment." And then she added, "Let's not talk about my illness. Tony told me about your daughter's pregnancy – when is the baby due?"

"In a month or so – I'm not looking forward to becoming a grandmother though. It reminds me that I'm getting old," Nora said and made Carole smile.

"I wish I had the time to see Paul's child. Ah…well, that's how it is – saves me the frustration of being called an old granny I suppose," she sighed and then smiled again.

"I just met Paul. I'm sure you're very proud of him."

"I am. I wouldn't have wished for a better son. Isn't he handsome? He looks just like his father, doesn't he?"

"I'm stunned. He looks so much like Waleed."

"I haven't heard anyone say that name for over 35 years. I haven't uttered it – not even once all these years. It's strange to hear it."

"It was really tough on you to deal with Waleed's suicide, I know. You felt betrayed that he left you on your own."

"As much as I loved him then to the point of adoration, I equally grew to hate him intensely. You think it's ridiculous to say that but I don't. It's two sides of the same coin."

There was a long silence.

"Nora, I wanted to see you to apologize to you for taking Tony away from you. I am ashamed – I truly am. I was very young then and frightened when I discovered I was pregnant after what Waleed did. I was lost and Tony was there for me. Can you forgive me?" Carole said, her voice shaking and her tears flowing again.

"I forgave you a long time ago, Carole. And now that I know Paul is Waleed's son, I'm glad I did. In any case, it was never your fault. Tony chose to be with you," Nora said, holding back her tears.

"I've thought about it so many times over the years. It must have been devastating for you. You were all alone in Paris when we left. I thought you'd never speak to us or contact us again."

"I did, didn't I? Our friendship could never be broken in the end even if I was angry with Tony. Let's forget about the past. Don't tire yourself anymore over this. I don't want you to feel uncomfortable when you're fighting this damned disease."

"I want to talk about it. I've buried it in my chest for 38 years. I've got to let it out. There are things you don't know and I owe it to you to tell you."

"What things are you talking about?"

"Weren't you ever curious about why Tony and I became so close?"

"It definitely did cross my mind. I thought it was because of Waleed's death and you needed someone to be beside you. Was I wrong?"

"You weren't. Tony was my shoulder to cry on – true. But that's not the only reason why he stayed with me."

"What do you mean?"

"Waleed was not the only one who was going through a deep depression before he took his life. I was, too. I was going through a nervous breakdown, Nora, and you were unaware of it. If it weren't for Tony, I would have committed suicide, too. He saved me. I owe him my life and the happiness that I experienced here in Canada."

Carole was out of breath. She now breathed very heavily and went all pale in the face.

"I'll call Tony or the nurse. We'll talk again later."

"Stop! Please, don't call anyone. I'll be alright. I have this all the time," Carole said and taking a deep breath, continued. "I was angry and devastated when Waleed died and when I found out I was pregnant with his child, I completely gave up on the will to live. I could never tell my parents about what had happened. I was in such a rage that the only way out was death for me. But Tony slowly changed my mind. He convinced me it was worth living and giving birth to the baby. He became my guardian angel. We developed a special bond between us and in his desire to protect me, mainly from myself, he married me. He is the reason I eventually loved Paul." Carole said, stopping at the end of each sentence for deep breaths.

"I don't understand Carole. Why wouldn't you want and love your child?"

Carole was now seriously out of breath. Nora quickly reached for the button next to the bed. As she did this, she felt Carole grab her arm with all the strength she could muster. She rang the alarm bell nevertheless and quickly turned around to look at Carole's face. Carole's dead eyes looked into hers.

"You need to know. You must know the truth. Waleed raped me the week before he killed himself," she said in a whisper.

A nurse and Tony arrived and Nora quickly left the room. A doctor turned up with a couple of nurses a few minutes later. Nora paced up and down the corridor for a good twenty minutes, her head trying to come to terms with what she was just told. The medical staff finally left the room. Tony followed them out.

"Is she okay?"

"Yes, they stabilized her condition. She's breathing normally. They put her on the assisted breathing machine again."

"Oh, thank God! It must have been the result of emotions on seeing me. I'm so sorry," Nora said.

"She's had shortness of breath almost every day. Don't blame yourself. Her breathing is stable now and the nurse on duty will check on her. Let's get something to eat and I'll have to take you to the hotel afterwards. You must be completely exhausted."

They had dinner at a local downtown eatery and Tony took her to the hotel. They didn't talk about Carole. All Tony asked was whether she had a good conversation with Carole. She said she did and fell silent. She had to process the secret that was kept from her for almost forty years. She couldn't talk about it casually in a restaurant.

When he said goodbye to her at the hotel, Tony asked if she wanted to see Carole again the following day. She said she did.

"I'm going back to the hospital now. I sleep in Carole's room almost every night now. I'll pick you up at 10 am then," Tony said and gave her a hug.

Nora couldn't focus on unpacking her suitcase. She thought of Waleed. She always believed she was right then. She knew he was suffering from depression and needed treatment but could never imagine he would hurt Carole, the person he loved the most, that way. What a tragic ending to an enviable love story. But why did Tony want to protect Carole so badly? Did he always fancy Carole secretly? He could have confided in her like he always did when there were difficult times. Why didn't he do that with Carole's situation? She could have helped Carole in her pregnancy even if Tony had to leave Paris for Canada. She would have gladly taken that responsibility. Why did Tony feel that the only way to protect Carole was to marry her? Nora didn't have the answers to her questions and it was unlikely that she would get them from Carole. After today's stressful conversation with Carole, she didn't want to cause her more discomfort by asking questions about the painful past.

Tony was late to pick her up the next morning. She didn't mind – she found a comfortable armchair in the lobby of the hotel and waited. Tony turned up an hour late. He looked terrible. He hadn't shaved or changed his cloths. His eyes were bloodshot.

"I'm really sorry. I'm very late. And I couldn't call."

"It's alright. You look terrible though. You look like you haven't slept all night. What's wrong – is everything okay?"

"Carole took her last breath this morning. She died in my arms," he said, his voice shaking.

"Oh God! I'm so sorry," said Nora and started tearing up.

"I was expecting this, but didn't think it would happen so quickly. It's as if she was waiting to see you – like she ticked all the things she wanted to do before she left this world, like having a bucket list. You were the last person she desperately wanted to see one last time," he said and seeing Nora's tears, he added, "Don't blame her. I'm glad you granted her one of her last wishes."

"I understand, Tony, you don't have to justify anything," Nora said, wiping her tears.

"I need to go back to the hospital. Paul's waiting for me. There's some paperwork to be taken care of. I'll come back at 5."

"Are you sure? Don't worry about me. You may want to be with Paul or want to be on your own today."

"Paul has to be in New York tonight for a recording which can't be postponed. And I certainly don't want to be alone. We'll talk later," he said and was gone.

———※※———

The week before Waleed's death

Carole looked out of the window in Waleed's dorm room. She could only say what she had to say with her back turned to him. She couldn't bottle it in anymore. She had kept mum and not told Tony or Nora about the countless arguments she'd had with Waleed in the last two months during which he'd turned violent. Waleed had slapped her on two occasions and one time pushed her away so hard she'd fallen and bruised her arm. Now, she knew she had lost all her patience. She had to do something drastic.

"I don't want to sound like I'm nagging again, but we can't go on like this," she started. "You're permanently depressed and you won't let anyone help you. It's been over a year since we came to Paris and you're still like this. I can't let you destroy yourself and me with you. You have to find a way of snapping out of this depression. You need to see a psychiatrist – you're deeper and deeper into this depression of yours. If you don't, I'm leaving you."

"What did you say? Stop talking nonsense this very minute."

"I'm serious this time, Waleed. I can't take it anymore."

"How many times do I have to tell you 'I love you'? Isn't my love enough for you? Don't do this to me."

"You don't get it, do you? I want a normal relationship – not a relationship with a self-destructing entity or a ghost."

"The hell with you, Carole, turn around and look at me!" He yelled.

"Let's break up!" She yelled back turning around and facing him.

He was so angry that his eyes seemed to be bulging out of their sockets. He was fuming. He didn't move for a few seconds. And then suddenly he lunged forward and grabbed her violently. He slammed her on the bed. He pinned her down and started kissing her. She struggled and tried to push him away as hard as she could. He then firmly locked the upper part of her body with one arm and with the other pulled her skirt up with such force that he tore it, punching her knee at the same time. The excruciating pain paralyzed Carole. He didn't stop even when she begged him to stop. He was someone else – not the Waleed she loved. He only loosened his grip when he'd finished. She was crying. She hastily got up and ran out of the room before he could gather his strength to stop her.

CHAPTER 23

TONY

When he'd finished all the paperwork that had to be done at the hospital and the arrangement of keeping Carole's body at the morgue, Tony drove to the house he had shared with Carole for over 30 years. There was an eerie silence in the house as he went in. Everything was in its place though: the books, the artefacts they had collected on their travels, the little knick-knacks that Carole used to decorate their lounge and kitchen with, the family photos displayed on the mantelpiece. Carole did the dusting and cleaning diligently every week. Sometimes she'd still be at it on his return from work and she'd say, 'I know the dust and these objects would still be here after I'm dead and gone, but I can't help it. I've got to clean the place.'

Tony now found himself sitting in Carole's armchair. He ran his fingers up and down the arms of the chair. His tears began to flow in abundance. He hadn't cried like that at the hospital. In the early hours of the morning, he'd shed a few tears when he knew Carole was no longer with him. He had then gently caressed her head and kissed her hand before calling the nurses in.

Carole had been his friend and companion for a lifetime and now she was no longer there. He knew he'd get used to being alone as time passed. But at that very moment, it was hard to accept she would not be appearing at the door, back from her visit to the hairdresser's or the nail parlour and showing her newly done fingernails with one or another shade of red that she liked. Tony felt satisfied with himself for having given her a normal life – a normal life with a husband, a healthy and intelligent son, a nice house – everything that she wanted in this life. And he remembered the words she repeated when they first settled in Canada, 'we were destined to spend this life together.' Was the reason really their destiny? He still wasn't sure. What he was sure of was that they tried to make their life together the best they could have had. He eventually got up to take a shower and change his clothing. He shouldn't be late this time to see Nora at the hotel.

⚎⚎

Nora was waiting for him at the spot he'd met her previously in the hotel lobby.

"Are you okay? Can I do something for you? Can I help in any way?"

"Thanks, but everything's been taken care of. It's been very difficult today," he said, "but I'm alright now."

"Shall we go to a quieter place for coffee? I'm not really hungry yet. The hotel café-bar at the back of the lobby has a subdued and calm atmosphere."

The first thing Nora said when they chose a corner table was to ask about the funeral. "It won't take place for another ten days to two weeks. We'll see how it goes and we'll have to wait for her family members to arrive from Australia. You can book your flight back to Paris whenever you wish. You've got to get back to work."

"Yes, I need to be back at work in four days' time. I'd taken a week off to come here."

"Nora, I'd like to thank you again for coming to see her one last time," Tony said and looked at Nora's face. She nodded and looked at him affectionately. It was the same look of all those years ago – the body ages but feelings do not, Tony thought. He had suppressed his feelings for Nora for so many years that he felt awkward now. He needed to get rid of his awkwardness by making light conversation.

"Did you know that you were very popular with boys back in Beirut?"

"What?"

"A lot of boys were interested in you. Some of them approached me, knowing I was friends with you. They wanted me to act as a go-between. But you were only interested in your studies, in music, and dreams of travelling. You were not aware of how attractive you were to the opposite sex."

"So why didn't you tell me? Why didn't you introduce those boys to me?"

"Why? I wanted you all to myself," he said and smiled.

Nora didn't respond. She took a sip of her coffee and looked at the empty space in front of her. She then excused herself and went to the washroom. A painful memory now emerged in Tony's head. He recalled the university restaurant incident in Paris when he and Carole came face to face with Nora unexpectedly. He hadn't visited Nora or called her in two weeks and knew she was deeply hurt when she saw him with Carole. It was written all over her face. It broke his heart into pieces to have hurt her like that, but there was nothing he could do about it.

Tony noticed Nora's stern face when she returned.

"Tony, I'm stupefied. I never expected to hear what I heard from Carole yesterday in all my life – may she rest in peace," she said earnestly. "Did you marry Carole because she was raped by Waleed and was carrying his child?" she then said bluntly but very quietly.

"Carole told you about how Waleed forced himself on her."

"Yes."

"It's more complicated than that but yes, if you want to put it in a nutshell. Try to put yourself in her shoes for one moment – I did then and I was terrified. The person she loved more than anything else in the world betrayed and hurt her. She was emotionally completely shattered. When it happened, she ran to me. I had to deal with the anger, weeping, and utter despair. There was no one else who knew both of them as well as I did. I went to see Waleed the following day, but he was remorseless. I realized their relationship was, like a precious vase, broken into a thousand pieces and there was no way of gluing the pieces back together. The shock of his suicide, and even more so when she found out she was pregnant, made her suicidal."

"Did you ever think of me when you made the decision to take control of Carole's life? You always asked for my opinion on matters back then. You were always hesitant when it came to making choices. Why didn't you come to me? We could have solved the problem differently."

"First of all, I could not report Waleed for what he had done, could I? He was my close friend. And who would have believed Carole? She was his lover. Everybody knew it. It wasn't like how rape is reported these days – not even in France back then. You should know that. And things took a different turn when Waleed committed suicide."

There was a long silence. Tony was certain Nora was computing and analysing everything she'd heard so far.

She finally said, "You mean Carole was emotionally so devastated and weak that you had to do something drastic? And, basically, threw away the feelings we had for each other because you thought I could handle your loss?"

"You were always the strongest among us. I knew you would be able to continue your life without me. I knew I would never be able to get over you but you could."

"Is that what you thought? Is that why you accused me of having another boyfriend the last time we saw each other in Paris?"

"I was hesitant at the beginning to make a decision on whether or not to marry Carole. I had not seen you for three weeks and went to the Armenian House one evening – sort of a cry for help if you want. But as I approached the building, I saw you with that German exchange student. He was talking to you and then he held your hand. You didn't push him away. You even allowed him to kiss you on the cheek before saying goodbye. I immediately turned around and went back to my dorm."

"And based on one incident, you decided to forget what we had. And after ignoring me for weeks on end, you had the cheek to pass judgment."

"That proved to me how strong you were, emotionally, I mean. But that was not the actual reason I took the decision to marry Carole. There are other reasons I cannot divulge that made me do it."

Tony looked at Nora. She was staring at him as if trying to read his mind. No. He could not let that happen. He'd said too much already. This is why he'd dreaded meeting her as much as he longed to see and be with her again. She had a way of disarming him. He should fight her curiosity with all his ability and strength.

"I've got an important favour to ask of you. But let's get something to eat first. I'll take you to a nice French restaurant in Hess Village, the oldest part of town with quaint old houses," he said although he didn't feel hungry one bit. He hoped she'd focus on the favour rather than continue the conversation they were having.

"Okay, let's go," she said cheerfully to his relief.

Being a weekday, the French restaurant had only one other table occupied. They ordered some wine and cold cuts because neither felt like eating anything.

"What's this important favour you want me to do you?"

"It's a lot to ask but you're the only one who can do it for me. I thought about it when I went home this afternoon and Carole was no longer there. I felt I now only have you in this world," he said, hesitating to continue. A few seconds later, he started, "Carole will be buried here. I've purchased a plot. A place that has green lawns and flowers – that's what she always said she wanted. But when I die, I want to be cremated. I want you to scatter my ashes beneath a pine tree in Lebanon. You know how much I love pine trees. I have never asked for anything grand or special for myself in this life. My only desire is to rest under the shade of a Lebanese pine tree."

"Are you serious?"

"I am. I want to go back, even in the form of ashes, to my birthplace. When I am sad or grieving like now, my sadness disappears when I imagine the smell of those old pine trees. That's where I want to end up."

"I don't understand. What nonsense is this? You still have plenty of time to live. Why are you thinking about death? And why do you want to be cremated? I know it has become a common practice in the West, but it's such an alien concept for someone who was brought up in the Middle East."

"I'm serious, Nora. It's my only wish. I don't want anyone to attend my funeral or to cry for me. I could never return or visit Lebanon without feeling guilty," he said and then controlling his emotions, he added, "I mean, I lived but my best friends died. I want to be able to go back there when I'm dead – one final time, free of all mortal constraints. Do you understand?"

"I'm trying to. But why me? Why don't you ask Paul to do it?"

"Frankly, I don't want Paul involved in this. He has never been to Lebanon and has no emotional ties to the place. He would never in a million years comprehend my yearning to have my remains, my ashes, rest there. It's difficult for me to express my thoughts, Nora. Let me say this: I'll have to re-write my will and make sure that everything is taken care of and everything you have to do is facile if you say yes. I never thought Carole would pass away before me.

You might think I'm being capricious or pretentious asking you to do something like this, having been away from you for almost forty years. But that's not the reality. For me you are the only person I trust my life or death with."

"Okay, stop, stop! Don't say anymore."

Tony looked into Nora's eyes. Her tears were welling but he could tell she was determined not to let them fall.

"If you can't do it, I'll understand. I will, truly," he said, regretting having put her under such pressure.

"Can you give me some time to think about it?" she finally said and asked if they could leave the restaurant.

Tony drove her to the hotel.

"I'll cook you dinner tomorrow. I'll pick you up in the evening," Tony said.

"Fine – I'll book my flight for the day after tomorrow," she told him before leaving the car.

Tony drove home, but when he parked the car, he didn't feel like going in. He re-started the car and went round and round the suburban neighbourhood. He went through the streets where there were the modest houses and then those that had the big houses with their lights shining on the vast grounds that surrounded them. He circled the neighbourhood again and again. And he finally found himself in front of his house. He stayed in the car. He should never have asked her. He now regretted it because he felt guilty. She'd already granted Carole her wish. Why did he have to ask more of her? He put his head on the steering wheel and remembered the last and painful encounter he had with Nora in Paris.

One evening made of pink and blue mystique,
We exchange a unique lightening,
Like a long sob, all charged with goodbye
from "Death of the Lovers" by Charles Baudelaire (trans.
from the French by the author)

"You're here at last! I thought I'd never see you again," Nora said, frowning, when she opened the door. She was wearing her pyjamas and had her hair tied up. "Wasn't expecting anyone to come round this evening," she said, still frowning and then fell silent. Tony understood she was upset with him and she was sulking.

"I'm sorry I couldn't come to see you sooner. How are you doing?"

"Absolutely fine," she said in a sarcastic tone.

"I've come to tell you something you won't be pleased about," Tony said firmly but he felt his stomach churning.

"Is that so? Nothing is going to shock me after what Waleed did."

"I'm leaving for Canada very soon."

"I was expecting you'd tell me this sooner or later. So, what's not to be pleased about? I know you're determined to go. Is this why you have been ignoring me since Waleed died? Was it some sort of training to prepare me for your departure?"

"No. I'm not going alone. I'm taking Carole with me."

"Are you pulling a prank on me? What's the meaning of this? Please, Tony, be serious and tell me what's going on."

"I'm marrying Carole and taking her with me to Canada."

They were standing in the middle of Nora's small room and Nora froze. Her big eyes got bigger and bigger and then she slapped him.

"Why are you doing this to me, Tony? What's wrong with you?"

"Calm down, Nora. I want you to listen to what I have to say. I developed feelings for Carole after Waleed passed away and we're getting married and leaving for Canada soon."

"Traitors! Both of you need to see a shrink. You're all gone mad!" She shouted and threw herself on her bed and started crying.

"Sit up, Nora! Please listen to me," Tony pulled one of her arms and made her sit up properly on the bed. He sat next to her.

"You're dumping me for her," she said, wiping her tears. She then started to laugh hysterically.

"Stop laughing, Nora, and hear me out. What you and I had was a beautiful phase in our lives but it could not last," he said, trying to convince himself that the words coming out of his mouth were true.

"Don't make me laugh again, Tony. You sound so insincere."

"You don't need me. You've got another boyfriend already – the German exchange student," he said, not looking at her.

"So now you're accusing me of cheating on you! What a convenient way of justifying your own behaviour."

"I'm not justifying anything. I'm telling you frankly what I've done and what I'm going to do."

Nora started to cry again but she drummed up the courage to say something he was not expecting to hear. It was her last and only weapon against him.

"You're a fool. Don't you know I love you? I've always loved you."

Tony knew if he stayed one minute longer in that room, he would lose all his self-control and she would win. He didn't respond to her and he swiftly left the room without looking back. Had he lost his composure, he would have hugged and comforted her. He would have wiped her tears and kissed her. He would have told her he adored her and would love her to his dying day. But he didn't. He had decided she was better off without him. He would spare her the burden he was carrying on his shoulders.

CHAPTER 24
THOU SHALT NOT KILL

Summer 1976

Waleed was high. He had smoked hasheesh all day and missed Carole. Her sister was getting married and would be immigrating to Australia with her husband right after the ceremony in Beirut. Carole had told him that she would not be able to come round for five or six days. She'd be tied up with all the preparations for the wedding and the imminent departure of her sister. Ever since Carole's abortion, Waleed found himself missing being with her every moment she wasn't there. He'd become so impulsive that the only way out was for him to smoke constantly. He couldn't explain it clearly in his head, but he was obsessed with her – all he could think about was Carole. And every time he was alone, he felt panic attacks coming on, accompanied by resentment over the issue of Carole's abortion. He tried to ignore those feelings but to no avail. He needed fresh air to clear his mind. The evening was drawing to a close and he decided to go for a walk. He hadn't been out in days. He should go out. He got dressed and then remembered the handgun. That's what he needed to take with him – just in case. He squeezed it on his side – between his jeans and his waist but didn't feel the metal's coldness when it touched his skin. He wore a loose, large shirt. There was a Druze checkpoint down his street and another one manned by another faction – he couldn't remember who – two blocks away. If anyone was going to give him trouble, he'd be armed and ready for it. He went past the Druze checkpoint and the armed guys with days-old stubbles and beards were just settling on makeshift stools for their evening coffee or tea. They all seemed in a good mood. They greeted him and let him through. Waleed didn't know which way to go after that. He decided to take a right turn. He went past two blocks thinking he might come upon another checkpoint but there was none. He needed fresh air. He should walk towards the sea, past the American University campus, to the Beirut Lighthouse. He could then descend the hill to the sea.

He wasn't aware of how long it took him or how he got to the Bliss Street Gate of the American University, but he was happy he was on the right track. He walked past the campus walls, but the evening traffic with taxis and shared taxis honking bothered him immensely. It was as if the sounds were getting amplified in his head. He had to stop the noise in his head. He crossed the street and took his first left into a side street. It was much quieter there and there was no car traffic. He went through one quiet side street after another and thought he was nearing the lighthouse. That's when he spotted the sign. He recognized the name. It was the name of the doctor who had performed the abortion on

Carole. It hit him right between the eyes. He stopped. The sign was dangling from a wrought iron structure in front of the building. He peered through the wrought iron gate which was left ajar. The forecourt had two big trees with branches covering part of the building. Four small steps led to the entrance. It was already getting dark and he noticed someone put the lights on. They were the clinic lights on the ground floor.

He tiptoed and approached the side window of the clinic. The neon lights of the clinic were powerful enough for him to make out the figure of a man clad in a white doctor's coat through the openings of the blinds. All of a sudden, he felt a surge of anger in him. He decided to confront the man. He went in. The door of the clinic was open. There was no one at the reception desk. The doctor's surgery door was open, too. He headed towards it quietly. When he entered the room, the doctor was standing up. He had removed his white coat and seemed to be getting ready to leave. A bald man of early 40's, who probably looked older than he was, stared at him.

"The clinic's closed. I'm leaving. You really need to make an appointment for your wife with the receptionist first, young man," he said.

"You killed my child," Waleed yelled. What an arrogant piece of shit, Waleed thought, and felt so angry that he immediately grabbed the gun he was hiding and pointed it towards the doctor.

"Calm down now. Let's talk," the doctor said softly and then froze with a terrorized look on his face.

"Calm down, calm down, what a joke! You need to promise never to perform illegal abortions again or else I *will* kill you!" Waleed shouted putting his finger on the trigger.

"Okay. I will. Calm down and stop pointing that gun towards me."

"Say it again! 'I will never perform illegal abortions again.'" Waleed was seething with anger and his hands began to shake.

Before he could answer Waleed, the bullet hit the doctor. He collapsed behind his desk. Blood splattered on the white wall behind him where he was standing a second ago.

Waleed's hands began to shake even more, but he managed to hide the gun again somehow and ran out of the room and the building. It was already dark by now. He didn't see anyone around. He crossed the street and turned right into another side street and disappeared.

Waleed had such an awful headache when he opened his eyes that he thought his head was going to explode. Someone was banging on his door. He got up and opened the door. It was Tony. Why on earth was he there?

"Don't you remember? You called me very late last night and begged me to come. You said it was an emergency. I crossed the Green Line very early this morning. What's the problem?"

Waleed went and sat on the sofa without answering him.

"What's so urgent that you wanted me here without delay?"

Waleed rubbed his eyes and squinted. His face now took the expression of someone trying very hard to remember something.

"Shit, shit, shit! I think I killed someone with the gun last night," he finally said.

"What?! What happened? How?"

"I killed him."

"Who? Waleed, you're not making sense."

"I killed the doctor – the abortion doctor. I went for a walk and ended up near the clinic. I just wanted to threaten him – vent my frustration. He killed my baby. The gun went off and he collapsed."

"For God's sake, Waleed. Were you high on hasheesh? What have you done?!"

"I'd been smoking all day. I don't know how I ended up there or why I was so angry at this man."

"Are you sure you pulled the trigger and you're not imagining things?"

"My hands were shaking – I've had the shakes lately and it just went off. I didn't mean to pull the trigger."

"Are you sure he's dead? Maybe he isn't. Maybe you just injured him. Where did you hit him?"

"I don't know. He just collapsed behind his desk. I saw blood. I ran out of the clinic as fast as I could."

"What the fuck, Waleed! You've got yourself in real trouble. If what you're saying is true, I can't really help you on my own. We need Ramzi's help. We need to call him *now*!"

Ramzi turned up an hour later. They told him what had happened.

"It's a good thing your parents are abroad, Waleed. Phew! That's a relief. But before we do anything, we need to make a pact. The three of us have to swear we will not divulge any of this to any other living soul," Ramzi said earnestly.

They each swore and the pact was sealed.

"I want Waleed to swear again when I'm sure he's sober. Tony, make sure he doesn't touch the hasheesh stuff. His oath is worthless if he's on a high."

"I promise," said Waleed sheepishly.

"Okay. What I'm going to do is find out if there are any reports of a murder or assault with a gun. Let me see the gun," he ordered Waleed.

After checking it, he said, "There's a bullet missing." And turning around to Tony, he gave another order. "Hide it somewhere for the time being. We don't have much time. Stay put. Don't go anywhere. I'll be back as soon as I can."

Waleed lay on the sofa now without saying anything. Tony paced up and down the length of the living room, feeling totally helpless and depressed. His mind racing, he suddenly thought of Nora.

"We've got to get rid of that gun whether you killed the man or not. It could be traced back to Nora. She bought it with Ramzi. There are witnesses. Are you listening to me?"

There was no reply from Waleed. Tony went over and poked him. Waleed was drenched in sweat and had passed out. Tony got some water and splashed his face, shaking him. Waleed eventually came to.

"You probably haven't eaten properly in days. You've got to eat!"

"I have no appetite."

"Waleed – for heaven's sake – you've got to be strong here. You've got to pull yourself together for all our sakes. Promise me!"

"I promise," Waleed said after staring at Tony's face with blank eyes.

Ramzi returned bearing bad news. The doctor was dead he reported. He said he'd got the information from a Shiite reporter from the Imam's entourage who specialised in crime reporting and had close ties with the police. He said the news was already published in the reporter's newspaper – a small paragraph in the crime section. But he said it would maybe make the headlines the next day.

"I'll turn myself in," Waleed said with determination.

"You will do no such thing. Have you ever visited a Lebanese jail? I have. The living conditions are so bad in there, and probably worse now with the civil war, that no man can come out of there alive or sane. Can you survive the trickle of water for washing, the dirt, and sometimes the beatings? I don't think you can, Waleed," said Ramzi.

"I won't allow you to turn yourself in," Tony shouted. "Think of Nora and Ramzi. They're the ones who bought the gun. They'll be accused as your accomplices. I won't allow you to get them involved – whatever the cost, you hear?"

"Do you remember if you touched anything at the clinic? Even with the civil war on, the police still use the standard finger print techniques. Did you touch the man's body?" Ramzi inquired.

"He can't even remember where he hit the man," Tony said angrily.

"I didn't touch anything. I'm sure of that. I don't know where the bullet hit him. He fell behind the desk and I ran out of the place."

"The bullet went through his cheek and out behind the skull," said Ramzi.

"Jesus!"

"Stop it, Tony! Let's keep calm here. No need to panic," Ramzi said.

"So, what do we do now?" Waleed asked, looking like a zombie.

"Here's what I'm going to do. Give me the gun. I will have it melted in acid so there will be no trace of it. I know people in the southern suburbs who can do it."

"But you're risking a lot. Won't people ask questions?" Tony said, looking concerned.

"No. There's a huge wall of silence with my people. And the police don't go near those areas," Ramzi said with confidence, and then added, "in any case, as long as it's not traceable, there's no problem."

"But someone might have seen Waleed come out of the clinic," Tony said.

"It was already dark when I went inside and pitch dark when I left that building. The forecourt didn't have any lights. I'm certain there was no one around. I remember that very clearly."

"Okay. Now for the good news – I got this from the journalist reporting what was being said by the police. This doctor had performed hundreds of illegal abortions. The police didn't know much about his activities, but they got this after their initial investigation into the murder. So, there are hundreds of possible suspects – lovers, fathers, and brothers – who may have wanted to kill the doctor in revenge. But we have to be careful just in case someone spotted you, Waleed. You were high on hasheesh and you may not have noticed. We need to be level-headed here and act quickly. You've got to leave West Beirut. Can you take him back to East Beirut with you?" Ramzi asked Tony.

"Yeah – I can."

"Weren't you leaving for Paris soon anyway? You'll have to leave earlier than planned. Get out of Lebanon as soon as possible."

"What about Carole? We were supposed to leave together and she can't leave right now. Her sister's getting married in a few days," Waleed said.

"Look – I'm not asking you to change any of your plans. Just leave sooner. I'd say within one week. Find an excuse to tell Carole you've gone to East Beirut with Tony. Once you decide on your final date of departure with Nora, I promise I'll get Carole over to the Green Line to join you."

"I owe you big time, Ramzi," was all Waleed said before Ramzi left.

It was very late that very same night when Ramzi called them. And as agreed, he said, "I won't be coming with you. Good luck! Have a good trip!" That was the secret code they'd agreed he'd use. It meant the gun had been destroyed.

Tony let out a sigh of relief and urged Waleed to pack his suitcase immediately. Feeling exhausted, Tony finally sat down in one of the armchairs but as soon as he did this, he felt nauseous. He rushed to the toilet and threw up.

The following morning Waleed called Carole and told her that he was going to East Beirut with Tony.

"Why?" she said, surprised.

"It's an emergency. My mother's relative is ill in hospital in East Beirut. She called me last night and said I should go and visit a few times on her behalf. I'll be staying at Tony's and I'm taking my suitcase with me. As soon as we decide on the date of our departure for Paris with Nora, I'll let you know. It'll be within the coming week. So, get ready. I think your sister's wedding and all of that would be over by then. I won't cross back to West Beirut. Ramzi was here last night and he said he'll take the responsibility of getting you to the Green Line on the set date. Are you okay with that?"

"Yes," she said, a bit perplexed. She'd never heard Waleed put as many sentences together in such a short time before. "See you soon then. I love you!" She said before hanging up.

Tony and Waleed crossed the Green Line that morning. Neither of them had the appetite to chat on the way. When they got to Tony's place, Tony parked the car and was just about to open the car door when he heard Waleed say, 'How can I go on living? I've killed a man.' But Tony didn't have the opportunity to respond to his statement. He watched Nora walking towards the car, smiling.

CHAPTER 25
NORA

Nora got out of Tony's car in the driveway of Tony's house. From the outside the house looked impressive, surrounded by a lush green lawn. She noticed the flower bushes scattered here and there. This is where they lived for all those years – a typical North American, large, comfortable house in an up-market neighbourhood.

"The house is quite spacious and it also has a large basement that Carole decorated over the years. There's a vast garden out back," Tony said opening the front door.

"Nice!"

"I've got dinner ready. Have a seat in the living room while I heat it up. Won't take long," Tony said and left for the kitchen.

Nora examined her surroundings. She felt Carole's presence in every corner of the room. The living room was not decorated to her European minimalist taste at all – very North American. But Carole must have loved the place and was proud of it. Tony brought her some wine and then they sat in the kitchen to have dinner.

"Oh, hummus with roasted pine nuts on top for starters – that's my favourite! You remembered!"

"How can I not remember? I know how much you loved pine nuts and you obviously still do," Tony said and then added, "I must come clean though – I didn't make the hummus from scratch. It's available here at the market. I just added the roasted pine nuts on top."

They both laughed and when the dinner was coming to an end Nora felt the urge to say something she'd always wanted to tell Tony.

"I wonder what our lives would have been like if the two of us had stayed together."

"I'm sorry we had to part ways," Tony said. He sounded like someone full of remorse.

"I'm sorry I said that. Forget it."

"How can I forget? Do you know how difficult it was for me to let you go?"

"Then why did you?"

"I need to tell you what happened again," Tony said, taking a deep breath. "The night Carole was raped she ran to my room crying. I consoled her and let her sleep in my room as my roommate was away. The next day I had a talk with Waleed, but he was his usual nonchalant self. I believed he was unaware of what he'd done. Carole swore she'd never want to see him again. She was in a hell of a state and stayed in my room for that whole week, not leaving the room once. When Waleed committed suicide, she was a complete mess – I can't really describe the horribleness of it in words. She thought it was because of her that he did what he did – out of guilt. I could not leave her alone. I thought she might do the same. One moment, she was full of hatred towards him, and the next she felt terribly guilty for having caused his death. As the weeks went by, she became more and more dependent on me. I knew it, and I let it happen. And then when she found out she was pregnant with Waleed's child, she went nuts. At first, she talked about suicide again. I tried very hard to talk her out of it. I succeeded but then she said she wanted to abort it – to erase the memory that he hurt her and left her all alone to deal with the aftermath. I went to the doctor with her convinced it was the right thing to do, but the doctor told her a second abortion would greatly reduce her chance of getting pregnant in the future. She hesitated and so did I, not knowing what to advise her to do. Eventually, I persuaded her to keep the baby. After all, Waleed was the love of her life. But I knew it was going to be very hard for her to be a single mother. I thought of her parents, her not being able to work and all of that, and the decision to marry her was my solution to the problem. We had grown very close to each other by then and it all happened naturally."

Nora didn't respond immediately to what she heard. She nursed her glass of wine for a long while.

"I'm not blaming you for having chosen her over me. I understand the circumstances now. But what hurts is that you didn't tell me any of this then. I was in love with you and I would have done everything I could to find a different solution to Carole's problem. I thought we were a team. But you never gave me a chance. You cut me off – just like that. You never truly cared about me like I did you – did you? I've thought about it all these past years and I've always come to the conclusion that there was infatuation or admiration but not love on your part. I'm sorry, I shouldn't talk about this at all – it's all too late now."

"You're wrong, Nora. I loved you but I never told you so," Tony said unexpectedly.

There was a long silence.

"I can't do what you've asked me to. I can't take that responsibility. I'm sorry. I'd better go back to the hotel now – thank you for dinner," Nora said breaking the long silence.

"Stay!"

"How can you ask me to stay? We have nothing more to say to each other."

"Please stay! I'm begging you. Don't leave – not just yet."

"You've kept me in the dark all these years. You're still hiding things from me – I know it, I feel it! Tony, I've done what I came here to do. I'm leaving now and you won't see me again."

"I swear I'm not hiding anything from you. Let's not part ways like this. Please, Nora..."

"You're lying. If you want me to be in your life, you need to tell me everything that you're hiding from me."

Nora stood up to leave but she stopped. Tony was crying. She'd only ever seen him cry like this once – when Michel died. He was crying like a child. It was as if he'd kept all the tears bottled up in his heart. Now, they came out like a torrent.

"Tony, please tell me what's bothering you. Please, don't leave me in the dark again. I can't stand it. I promise I won't blame you for anything. Tell me..."

"It's abhorrent what I'm going to say," he said, still in tears. There was no way of avoiding it now. He didn't want to lose Nora. She was a strong, independent woman – much stronger than the innocent girl he knew then. She was strong enough to walk away. He didn't want her to disappear from his life again.

"Please say it! It's me, your Nora."

"Waleed killed the abortion doctor in Beirut. And I covered it up for him and kept my mouth shut. I've kept the secret for all these years. I promised not to tell anyone, especially you. But I can't lose you again."

There was a long silence again. Nora stood there – stupefied.

"Did Carole know?"

"No, she didn't. I never told her. And I never told her that I was in love with you. She blamed herself all these years for having hurt you. She knew you'd fallen in love with me. And how could I tell her that Waleed had killed someone and that was the reason why he was emotionally so fragile before committing suicide? What was the use of telling her? That her son was the son of a murderer? You see how difficult it was and is for me to tell Paul who his real father is. It's a big stain on the life of a child who had nothing to do with it…" and he continued sobbing.

Nora, who was still standing, sat down again. "How and why did it happen?"

"Waleed was high on hasheesh. He was carrying the gun you purchased with Ramzi. Something evil directed him to the doctor's clinic and he shot him accidentally, killing him."

"Is this why both you and Waleed were so adamant on leaving Beirut quickly?"

"Yes. We wanted to get out of Lebanon as quickly as we could."

"What happened to the gun?"

"Ramzi got rid of the gun for us."

"So, he knew, but not Sana."

"Yes. And he took the secret with him and so did Waleed. It's only me left. We made a pact at the time – the three of us – not to tell anyone. But now you've forced me to break that promise. Now you know everything."

"I resented Waleed for committing suicide – all these past years I thought he was a coward. But now I feel sorry for him – he just couldn't live with the fact that he had killed someone even if he did it unintentionally. It drove him crazy to the extent that he ended up hurting the one he loved most. You should have told me all this then – not now. We could have faced everything together."

"I wanted to protect you from all the ugliness, Nora. What kind of life would you have had with someone who was akin to an accomplice to a murder? I had helped Waleed in covering up his murderous act. And although you warned me at the time about his mental state, I hadn't been aware of the degree of torment he was in to help him surmount it and to stop him from committing suicide. I was as guilty as he was. I couldn't let you know any of this. I needed to protect you with all the power I had. You had purchased the gun. I knew you too well then. I couldn't let you carry the burden of guilt – you were such an innocent, loveable young girl. I couldn't allow myself to let you have a murder on your conscience as well. It would have destroyed you and your life!"

"You deprived me of your love to stop me from feeling guilty..."

"It was the most difficult decision I had to take in my life. I had to run away from you reluctantly. Dealing with the guilt I felt was unimaginably hard and I wanted to spare you that burden. I knew I had to tell you if I married you. I couldn't let that happen. Do you understand now?"

"I really don't know if my life has been any better without you. What can I say – life has dealt us the cards it wants to deal us – it hasn't been easy for any of us, has it?"

"Will you forgive me?"

"Tony, I told this to Carole as well – I forgave her and you a long time ago. I loved you both and I always will. Let's never talk about this again."

Nora now watched Tony slowly get up from his seat. He walked towards her, looking straight into her eyes. As he approached her, he stretched his arms. She naturally moved towards him. He hugged her tightly and she reciprocated. But she knew she could not stay there forever. She had to leave.

"I need to go back to the hotel," she said, still hugging him. "Will you call a cab for me?"

"Why a cab? I'll drive you there and I'll pick you up tomorrow and drive you to the airport. When's your flight for Paris?" Tony said as he let go of her.

"My flight is very early in the morning. I don't want you to drive me back to the hotel or drive me to the airport. We'll meet each other again someday. I'm sure of it. But I'm no good at saying goodbyes. Please Tony, let's just say goodbye now."

When the cab arrived, Tony thanked her one more time with teary eyes. They hugged each other once more and Tony kissed her on both her cheeks before she went into the car.

"I'll think about what you asked of me. Give me a bit more time," Nora said before the cab moved.

⚜

It had almost been a month since Nora was back in Paris. She had text messaged Tony to say she had arrived safely but that was all the communication between them. She didn't feel like asking him about Carole's funeral. He hadn't written to her about it either. Nora had been so busy at work the past weeks that she fell asleep the minute her head hit the pillow. She was satisfied with things as they were in her workplace now – she didn't want to worry about her position in the company just yet. What she was anxious about was her daughter's pregnancy and the delivery date approaching.

And then she got the phone call from her daughter's partner one very early morning. He said her daughter had given birth to a healthy baby girl only half an hour earlier. She rushed to the hospital. Her daughter and the father of the baby were holding hands when she entered the hospital room. Her daughter looked fragile but her face was beaming with happiness.

"Did everything go well? Everything's alright?" Nora asked.

"Yes, Mum. We have a healthy baby girl. We haven't decided on the name yet," she said with a smile.

Nora approached her daughter and hugged and kissed her.

"Congratulations to both of you," she said, caressing her daughter's cheek. "I can't stay long. I've got to get to work. I'll be back in the evening. Can I see the baby?"

Nora's future son-in-law led her to the babies' ward. Her granddaughter was asleep in a little transparent crib. Nora pressed her cheek on the glass wall that separated her from her granddaughter. She ran her fingers up and down the glass barrier, tracing the contours of the baby's face, touching her closed eyes, the nose, and the lips. And the love she had for this little being was so powerful, it dizzied her. She felt the urge to hold her. 'I'll hold her later today,' she told herself but felt the impatience as she headed towards her car parked in the underground car park of the hospital.

She started the car but she didn't move. She stared out of the windscreen at nothing. She was nothing on this earth. They were nothing. She felt smaller than her granddaughter. In the vast universe, Nora felt she was smaller than a tiny spec. Insignificant as her life seemed, her expectations, her emotions, and her affection were so much bigger and more important than her mortal self. Her grandparents were survivors of genocide and had lived as refugees in a new country. She herself had arrived in France as a refugee of war. But she had kept on living like her grandparents did – giving life and the life she had given gave way to another new life.

She heard someone humming an old Lebanese Fairouz song – 'Visit me every year. It would be such a shame if you completely forgot about me.'* She looked around, but there was no one in the car park. She then began reciting one of the verses of a poem she'd learned a long time ago –
Beirut, in the Orient, is the last sanctuary

---

* Fairouz song lyrics (trans. from the Arabic by the author)

Where man can still wear the garb of light.**
She felt her lips. They were wet. She wiped them and her eyes. She now reached out for her phone. She looked for Tony's number and sent him a text message. Three words were all she typed. 'I'll do it'. She then put her foot on the accelerator and the car moved. She was in Basement 3. She'd always felt claustrophobic in basement car parks – dark, like she imagined tombs would be. The car began its ascent to the top floors. It twisted and twisted again, negotiating the narrow passageways, imprisoned by high walls, until it reached the exit level. The minute the nose of the car was out of the abyss, the sunlight blinded Nora. But she was not bothered by it – she welcomed it.

** from "Beyrouth" by Nadia Tueni (trans. from the French by the author)

Z. T. BALIAN

Born in Beirut to Armenian parents, Z. T. Balian is a multilingual French author who holds an MA in English Literature from the American University of Beirut. After a career as a lecturer at a number of Middle Eastern universities, during which she published several English textbooks, she now devotes her time to writing fiction and poetry. *Fallen Pine Cones* is her second novel. She published her debut novel, *Three Kisses of the Cobra*, in 2016. She writes poetry both in English and Armenian. *Waiting for Morning Twilight* (forthcoming, Summer 2023) is her collection of haiku poetry in English and her *199 Haiku Poems in Western Armenian* was published in 2022. Her haiku poems in Armenian are regularly published by *Hayeren Blog*, and her poetry in English has previously appeared in *Hope: An Anthology of Poetry* (2020) and *Setu Mag's Poetry: Western Voices* (2021, 2022, 2023). She currently lives in Istanbul and is working on a poetry book in English and a third novel.

Made in the USA
Las Vegas, NV
21 July 2023